The Lying Tree

The Lying Tree

Alexa Tewkesbury & Steve Legg

CanaanPress

CanaanPress

First printed in Great Britain in 2008 by
Canaan Press
5 Willowhayne Close
Angmering on Sea
West Sussex
BN16 1PF
office@canaanpress.co.uk
www.canaanpress.co.uk

The book imprint of
Matt's Canaan Trust
www.mattscanaantrust.com

British Library Cataloguing in Publication Data
A record of this is book is available from the British Library

ISBN: 978-0-9551816-3-4

Designed by Andy Ashdown
www.andyashdowndesign.co.uk

Illustrations by Nadia Chalk

Manufactured in Malta by Gutenberg Press Limited

For Jay, Amber, Emmie, Maddie, John and Lydia –
without you life just wouldn't be life.

With very much love
X

1

Truth and lies

"You still here?"

A grinning, freckled face was poking through the open window of the dusty 4 x 4 that had just pulled up. Jamie wobbled to a halt. He hadn't quite got the hang of the mountain bike he was riding. It was a Specialized Stumpjumper with twenty-seven gears. Jamie wasn't even sure it was his, but his own battered old bike seemed to have disappeared and he had to get home somehow.

"Thought you'd have gone right back to get sorted," Max continued.

Sorted?

"No, I..."

Jamie's voice trailed off. What could he say? He didn't have a clue what Max was talking about. Not only that but, any minute now, Max would spot the Stumpjumper. He'd know it wasn't Jamie's. Then there would be the inevitable question, "Where did you get that?" He was the first friend Jamie had made when he had started at Wellbridge Primary four months ago, and he never missed a thing. Jamie watched Max's eyes travel over the gleaming, red paintwork. He waited uncomfortably. He didn't know where the bike had come from himself so how could he explain it to someone else? But the question never came.

"Do you want a lift?" Max's mum was leaning across from the driver's seat. "You may as well. I'm just dropping all the gear round to your dad now."

All *what* gear? What in the world was going on?

Suddenly Maggie Renton was standing beside him with a hand on the saddle of the bike.

"Come on," she said cheerfully, "let's sling this on the rack."

Max looked at her, horrified.

"You don't 'sling' a Stumpjumper, Mum," he remarked.

Jamie watched in a daze as Mrs Renton wheeled the bike round the back of the jeep. Neither she nor Max seemed in the least surprised to see him riding it.

"Give us a hand then, Jamie," she chivvied.

He managed to help lift it onto the rack but then stood staring blankly while she did up the straps. She saw his face and smiled.

"My word, Jamie, you must have had a hard week! Go on, in you get."

Jamie hesitated.

"I need to get home," he murmured.

Mrs Renton laughed and opened the door.

"That's why I'm giving you a lift, silly!"

Max slipped through from the front to the back and strapped himself in beside Jamie.

"This is going to be so cool," he said eagerly. "Wait till you see my tent."

Jamie felt himself plunging deeper into confusion. Why did Max want him to see his tent?

"Where are we going?" he managed to ask.

"Er – hello?" Max frowned. "We're taking you home. Have you been in the sun too long or something? You're acting really weird."

Not half as weird as I'm feeling, Jamie thought.

Then it hit him.

In ten minutes it would all be over. Jamie didn't know *how* Max and his mum had discovered where he lived, but somehow they had. They would drive into his dismal little street and stop in front of his even more dismal little house. Max would look at him in disbelief and say, "What's this supposed to be? You told us you were a rich kid." And Jamie would say nothing because there was nothing to say.

The jeep headed up the hill out of Wellbridge. Beside him Jamie could hear Max jabbering away, but he couldn't make out the words. He felt numb. He'd tried so hard to keep everyone away but it hadn't worked. Now there were just moments left. Then he'd be uncovered for the desperate liar he really was.

* * * * * *

Until Jamie Bryce was nine years old, he had lived a happy, normal life. At least that's how it had felt. Every morning his dad went to work and his mum got on with looking after him. When he was old enough to start school, she would drop him off at the main door, disappear to her job as a home help, and always be back to pick him up at a quarter past three. They'd play games together and go shopping. It was Jamie's mum who had taught him to count and to read. It was his mum who had showed him how to tell the time.

When Jamie looked back, he couldn't remember any arguments. He couldn't remember his mum seeming sad or dissatisfied. But there must have been something badly wrong. One morning he woke up and she simply wasn't there.

She wasn't there ever again.

"It's nothing you've done," Jamie's dad had tried to reassure him. "She was unhappy, that's all."

But Jamie had his own ideas. Mums didn't just pack their bags and leave. There had to be a reason.

"She didn't love me enough," he told himself finally. "It's obvious. In fact she didn't love me at all."

A year and a half later, Jamie and his dad had moved away from their shattered life to try and start again somewhere new. Mr Bryce, a not very successful estate agent, took a job as another not very successful estate agent, and the two of them settled into an old, scruffy, two-bedroomed, terraced house on the edge of a small market town. Jamie began to go to school in the nearby village of Wellbridge.

"It's smaller than the ones in town," his dad said to him. "It'll be easier for you to make new mates there."

But Jamie wasn't sure he wanted any new mates. At eleven years old, he had become quite a loner. He was angry. He couldn't understand his dad. Why had he let his mum walk away? Why hadn't he gone after her to try and persuade her, force her even, to come home? His dad never seemed to show any spark. He had no energy. He was a dull, grey man who seemed to become duller and greyer with each passing week. Sometimes Jamie wasn't even sure he liked him that much.

Anyway, new mates would try to pry. He didn't want anyone else knowing that his mum left home because she didn't think he was worth staying for. He'd been through that at his other school. He couldn't stand any more talking behind his back or laughing about him. The worst fear of all was that someone might say, "Well, look at you. It's no wonder she left." Because that was what Jamie thought himself.

And that's how the lies all began. If Jamie kept himself to himself, if he didn't get involved with anyone and certainly kept his private life private, he could say anything he wanted. He could be anyone. He could invent an entire life. No-one would ever know the truth because he'd never let anyone get close enough to find out. It was brilliant.

Jamie lied about everything. He said he used to go to a posh school before they moved, with its own theatre and recording studios and sports complex. He said his father was a high-flying businessman who had lots of employees to look after. He even pretended to live in a big house on the far side of town, with a massive swimming pool in the acres of garden. After all, who'd ever know? He'd never invite anyone home, and as he could cycle to school or get the bus in bad weather, he'd never need a lift, so there wasn't much chance of anyone from school even seeing his dad, let alone getting into a conversation with him.

The biggest lie was the one about his mum. She never left. She was just away a lot because she had such an important job.

"I can't really tell you anything, though," Jamie

would say if anyone asked. "I'm not supposed to talk about it," which gave the impression that perhaps his mum was involved in something top secret and dangerous. Jamie didn't really care what people thought. Anything was better than telling the truth.

However, keeping himself to himself turned out to be much harder than he'd imagined. Max took him by surprise. Jamie hadn't expected to like anyone, but Max was different. With his round, freckled face topped with its rug-like mop of curls, he was always making Jamie laugh. He made him *want* to make friends. More than that, Max made him want to belong.

And being friends with Max meant being friends with Callum, Megan and Abby too, since they were Max's best mates. Callum was quieter and more serious than the others but easy enough to get on with, and Megan and Abby were proud to be the world's most unidentical twins. The only thing they appeared to have in common was the colour of their eyes. Both pairs were a piercing blue. Just like their dad's.

It wasn't that Jamie went out of his way to tell lies, but as the questions had come, the lies had followed. It didn't seem important to begin with. These were just kids in his class. What did it matter what he said? But as the friendships developed, the lying became more difficult. Jamie had to remember what he'd said. He had to be consistent.

Then, when he began to be invited back to his new friends' houses, the complications grew. There were parents to deal with, parents who were already curious about him because of the bits and pieces they'd picked up from their children – the bits and pieces of lies.

"It'll be fine," he kept telling himself. "Just don't talk about *you*, talk about *them*."

But it wasn't that simple. Wherever he went there were more questions, so there had to be more lies. How long would it be before he made a mistake, before he said the wrong thing? He could picture Max gaping at him, arms folded, the cheeky grin wiped from his lips.

One word out of place and Max would ask grimly, "What are you talking about, Jamie? That's not what you said yesterday."

The perfect lie was fast becoming a living nightmare. How could he keep it all going? How long would it be before his new friends discovered what a liar he really was?

So that Friday at the beginning of May, the last thing Jamie needed was Max, Callum, Megan and Abby pushing him into a night camping out in his garden.

"Oh, come on, Jamie," Max wheedled, "it'll be such a laugh."

"We can't," Jamie muttered in reply. "Mum's away."

"Your dad's there though."

"I don't know. We might be going off somewhere."

"Well, next weekend then," suggested Abby.

"We might be going off somewhere then as well." It was all Jamie could think of.

There was a pause and then, frowning, Callum said what the others were already thinking.

"You never invite us back to yours. Don't you want us there or something?"

Jamie forced a smile. "Of course I do. Camping out's a wicked idea. I just don't know what we're doing." He hesitated. "I'll talk to Dad and maybe give you a ring over the weekend."

Of course he wouldn't ring. There'd be nothing to say.

Pathetic. *He* was pathetic. How had he let himself get cornered like this? As he pushed his tired, old British Eagle mountain bike down to the school gates at the end of the day he thought, I wish we'd never moved here. All everyone wants to do is poke their noses in.

Jamie didn't feel like going home. Instead he turned in the opposite direction from town and headed towards the far end of Wellbridge. Where the houses thinned just past the park and the village finally petered out, a rough track led away from the road and up a hill. Jamie stood on the pedals and forced the worn-out wheels over the bumps and loose stones. He wanted to be on his own, away from everything. His dad wouldn't be home until nearly six o'clock. No-one would wonder where he was.

Half way up the hill was a gate with a stile where a footpath crossed the fields. Jamie pushed it open. It creaked painfully on ancient hinges as he wheeled his bike through the gap, then swung back behind him. He took a few steps along the footpath, but almost immediately veered off to the right across the field towards a derelict barn on the brow of the hill. Here he leaned the bike against one of the thin, rust-eaten panels of corrugated iron still clinging to the barn's battered skeleton. He was out of breath. It was a steep enough climb on its own without pushing a bike.

Suddenly he threw himself down on the grass, stretching out on his back, his eyes following enormous, white banks of clouds as they slid idly by. In complete contrast, inside his head his lies were zooming around haphazardly like clusters of bees in a wild flower garden. He closed his eyes. All he wanted was for everything to go away, for his life to be how it used to seem. Normal.

How long he lay there, Jamie wasn't sure. Perhaps he'd even fallen asleep. But all at once, there seemed to be light flickering inside his eyelids. He snapped them open. The late afternoon sun was still beaming down on him, but now its light was broken as it poured between the branches of a tree, filtered through faintly trembling leaves. Jamie squinted upwards and blinked.

It was a few seconds before it dawned on him.

I didn't lie down under a tree... Hang on. There aren't any trees in this field!

Hastily he propped himself up on his elbows. He hadn't moved. His bike was still

standing where he had left it and the empty barn
threw cool, grey shadows across the grass.

"Enjoy your nap?"

The voice came out of nowhere. Jamie twisted over
and scrambled to his feet. His heart thudded in his
chest. Was he trespassing? Perhaps he was. He'd
never really thought about it. This was just a place
where he liked to be.

A man was standing near him under the tree. He
was quite tall, but his body seemed lost inside a faded
linen suit that was far too big for him, the trousers
creased and baggy and the jacket swamping his
uncomfortably scrawny frame. He was smiling.

"It's all right, you needn't look so worried," he said,
clearly amused. "If you're trying to sort out your
problems, this is as good a place to come as any."

2

Pick your own destiny

Jamie said nothing. His instinct was to run. He certainly couldn't ride back down the hill. The stranger stood between him and his bike. He'd never be quick enough to dodge behind the man and grab it. He felt his muscles tense and took a few steps backwards. To his surprise, rather than get ready to chase after him, the man sat down.

"Go on, then," he sighed. "Run away if you like. I'm not going to stop you."

The man leaned back on his hands and stretched his legs out in front of him, crossing one sandaled foot over the other. Thin wisps of pale blonde hair trailed limply across his shoulders. The sun was behind him but, as he peered up at Jamie, his eyes looked so small he still seemed to be squinting.

"Can I get my bike, please?" Jamie asked quietly.

"Help yourself," the man replied. "Then you can be on your way home."

Jamie hesitated. Even from his sitting position, the stranger could still easily catch hold of him if he got too close. He was about to move one cautious step forward but the man's voice stopped him.

"Or you could stay and listen to what I have to say."

Jamie couldn't imagine the man having anything to say that he could possibly want to hear.

"I've got to get home," he muttered.

"Of course you have," the man nodded, "never mind," and Jamie had the feeling that that should have been the end of it, were it not for the man adding, "Well it was very nice to meet you, Jamie."

It stopped him dead. Ice cold began to prickle down his spine.

"How do you know my name?" Jamie gulped.

The man chuckled. "At least I know you're paying attention," he said. "But you see, Jamie, I know a lot more about you than just your name."

He paused. There was something unreal about the waxy paleness of his skin, as though it had never seen the sun.

Jamie swallowed hard. He wished he could just snatch his bike and hurtle away but somehow he couldn't move. He had to ask.

"What do you know?"

A satisfied smile stretched the man's thin lips for a moment, then vanished as his tiny eyes, like slivers of dark glass, were suddenly fixed on Jamie's.

He shrugged and said simply, "I know you're a

liar."

Jamie's mouth was so dry he thought his tongue would choke him. Here he was, alone in a field with a man he'd never seen before in his life, yet somehow this complete stranger knew all about him. He knew that whenever Jamie opened his mouth it was to make something up. He knew that not a word he spoke could be trusted. Jamie didn't know how or why but, incredibly, this decidedly odd figure, lolling on the grass in front of him, knew the truth.

"Come and sit down, Jamie," the man invited, still watching him closely. Jamie shook his head.

"What do you think of my tree?"

What? That was the last question Jamie expected. But, of course, *the tree!* In his panic he'd almost forgotten it. It shouldn't have been there. Yet, there it was, its arrival as weird and unexplained as that of the stranger.

The man reached back and placed a long-fingered, white hand on the smooth trunk.

"Isn't she beautiful?" he murmured. "Such a perfect shape."

The tree must have stood six metres high. Jamie's eyes travelled upwards to the gently domed crest. The curving branches were thickly dressed in lush, green leaves. It was magnificent. But where had it come from? How could there suddenly be a tree where there was nothing but a crumbling, old barn?

"You see, Jamie," the stranger continued, "the reason I know about you is because liars are automatically brought to my notice. Even the tiniest of lies can't escape me. But you, my boy, you have succeeded in weaving an entire existence and that is something worthy of my *full* attention."

Jamie had already gone cold. Now his blood seemed to freeze. Something was happening. Something he didn't understand. And the worst part was he somehow had to stand there and listen. His legs were locked rigid, rooting him to the spot.

"Who are you?" Jamie spoke the words so softly, he barely heard them himself.

"*Who* I am is neither here nor there," the man answered dismissively. "But *what* I am, now that's of far greater interest."

Jamie steeled himself. Was this man even human?

"All right," he asked slowly, "*what* are you?"

With a sudden burst of energy, the stranger clapped his hands together and sprang to his feet. Startled, Jamie stumbled backwards. The man bent towards him.

"Aha!" he cried, thrusting an excited, yellowish face close to Jamie's. "Now we're getting somewhere."

Jamie shrank away. The man straightened up, his beady eyes scanning the fields around them. For a moment he was silent. Then he lowered his head and spoke again.

"What am I? I'm the one who can help you. I can change your destiny."

His eyes narrowed and slid towards Jamie. The boy they scrutinised seemed very small and fragile.

"I'm the one who can give you your lie."

Jamie caught his breath. Supposing he was actually face to face with a raving nutter! Why hadn't he run away when he had the chance? More to the point, why had he come up here in the first place? How much worse was this day going to get?

The man leant towards him again and asked in a whisper, "Don't you want to know how?"

Jamie made no response, so he shrugged and continued airily, "Never mind, let me tell you anyway. I know how worried you are. I can feel it. You've been torturing yourself, wondering how long it will be before the truth comes out."

The man smiled. "I can spare you all of that. All that unnecessary misery. Just imagine. And it'll cost you nothing."

He turned to admire the tree behind him. He was clearly enjoying himself.

"You see, Jamie, this is the Lying Tree. It offers you the chance to live your lie. Pick a leaf, and your made-up world becomes your reality."

Jamie was right. This man *was* a nutter. A freak. How was he ever going to escape? He was fast, he knew that, but the stranger looked fairly athletic and he didn't much fancy his chances of reaching the field gate first. He glanced up. The man's eyes were burning into him again. He knew exactly what Jamie was thinking.

"Still want to run, eh?" he remarked flatly. "Pity. Still, perhaps it would be better if your friends did know the truth. I mean, let's face it, it's only a matter of time. Of course, they won't be your friends anymore. But then, you didn't want friends anyway. Did you?"

The man knew everything. Every thought. Every fear.

When he spoke again, his voice was softer, more persuasive.

"Why not give yourself a chance? Go on, pick a leaf. It's your lie, Jamie... Live it."

It made no sense. None of it. Jamie almost *wanted* to believe the man was mad. But even if he was, it still didn't explain the tree's sudden appearance out of nowhere or how the man seemed to know exactly what was going on in his mind. And then, what if the stranger wasn't mad at all? Could it really be that what he was saying was true?

Don't be an idiot, Jamie thought to himself, that

man's not right in the head. He can't be. How can it possibly be true? Play along. It's the only way out. Just play along.

He took a deep breath and looked the stranger full in the face.

"All right," he murmured, his voice low, trembling. "Which leaf do you want me to pick?"

"Oh no, you misunderstand," the man replied quickly. There was a spark of irritation in his eyes. "This has nothing to do with what *I* want. I'm simply offering you a way out. Whether you take it or not is up to you. Pick a leaf, don't pick a leaf. The decision's entirely yours."

Not *entirely*, Jamie thought. Alone in a field with the most bizarre person he had ever met, he didn't feel he had any choice at all.

He took a step towards the tree. The branches seemed to reach towards him, drawing him in as they offered their rich display of shimmering green.

But which one? Which one should he take?

Slowly, reluctantly, Jamie stretched out his hand. His fingers pushed their way into thick foliage, exploring the smooth, cool surfaces as they slipped over his skin. A shiver ran through him making the hairs on his arms and the back of his neck shoot bolt upright.

Do it. Just grab one.

"Wait!"

The man's voice pierced the stillness. Jamie was so taken aback, he almost leapt in the air.

"So sorry," the stranger said. The amused expression had returned to his face. "I'm always forgetting this part. There is just one more thing."

How could there possibly be anything else? Jamie thought.

"Once you've picked a leaf," the man continued hurriedly, "the lie is yours for seven days. If after that time you're completely satisfied, then you need do nothing. It's yours to keep forever."

He paused. "If, on the other hand, you're not happy and you decide you'd rather return to your old life, you are perfectly entitled to do so, provided it is within the seven days. However, this does require you to do something."

A lie on seven days' trial? Now Jamie began to think perhaps *he* was the one who'd gone mad.

"And what's that?" he found himself asking.

"You have four friends. Four good friends. Four friends you've been lying to since the day you met them. Should you wish to have everything back as it was, Jamie, not only do you have to tell them the truth, but they have to believe you."

Jamie stared at the stranger blankly. By now he was so confused he didn't know what was truth and what was lie, what was weird dream and what was reality.

"If they don't," the man shrugged, "well, by the end of the seven days, like it or not, your lie will be your life."

But Jamie was hardly listening any more. All he wanted was to get home.

His fingers closed round a leaf and he pulled. There was a soft snap. And it came away in his hand.

* * * * * *

Jamie flinched. Beside him in the jeep, Max had just elbowed him sharply in the ribs.

"What?" It was all he could manage.

"I *said*," Max repeated deliberately slowly, "I hope the weather stays good so we can use the pool."

"Yeah," Jamie mumbled. What else could he say? His head was buzzing so much he hadn't taken in a word Max had said. And even if he *had* been listening, Jamie had the distinct impression he wouldn't have known what on earth Max was talking about.

He was suddenly vaguely aware of the clicking of the jeep's indicator. They were about to turn right onto the main road down to town. Deal Street was only five minutes away. Deal Street, his shabby little house at number 15. And a lot of explaining. When Max knew the truth, he'd hate him.

Jamie leaned back and closed his eyes. If only he could work out what had happened. Perhaps he *had* fallen asleep as he lay on his back in the field. Perhaps he was *still* asleep and none of this was real. The trouble was, it didn't feel like a dream. He could picture every detail of the stranger's face, remember every word he had spoken.

Then there was the bike strapped to the rack at the back of the jeep. What had happened to his cranky old British Eagle? The moment he'd picked the leaf, the man had disappeared. He simply wasn't there any more. Jamie went to collect his bike to ride home, but the bike leaning up against the barn wasn't his. It was this Specialized Stumpjumper, almost brand new. Had the stranger left him this one in exchange for his own? No chance! No-one in their right mind would swap a top-of-the-range Stumpjumper for a clapped out British Eagle. But then there was nothing to suggest that the man on the hill *was* in his right mind.

Jamie hadn't known whether to take the bike or not, but he had to get home. He supposed he could always get his dad to take it to the police station later and just hope he didn't get accused of stealing in the meantime. But when Max saw the Stumpjumper, he never said a word. He wasn't even surprised.

Just before he'd slipped through the rickety gate and out of the field, Jamie had glanced back up the hill. The barn's rusting walls stood out, a distinct brownish-red against the fresh green of the new spring grass. He was wondering if the stranger might have reappeared. He hadn't. And this time the tree had vanished too.

Jamie's stomach twisted horribly. The jeep was nearing the garage. The turning was on the right. Right, then first left, and number 15 Deal Street was on the corner.

"I've got to get out. I feel sick." He said it so quietly, neither Max nor his mum seemed to hear.

He waited for them to brake, for the right indicator to click into life. Nothing happened. The bus they were following pulled into the stop opposite the turning, but the jeep just whisked by, gathering speed now that the road was clear. Jamie could hardly breathe. Was it going to be all right? Perhaps they didn't know where he lived after all, and he certainly wasn't going to tell them.

At the roundabout, the jeep slowed slightly then swept left away from the town.

Now where were they going?

A few minutes later, Max's mum flicked on the indicator again. Why? There weren't any junctions

ahead, not on this stretch of road. But before he knew
what was happening, they had made a right turn into
a wide gateway that Jamie didn't remember being
there. There were gate posts on either side, two
imposing columns with an angry stone lion crouching
on the top of each one, poised as if ready to spring at
anyone who was foolhardy enough to drive through
the entrance. The jeep began crunching along a
gravel driveway running between two lines of tall
hedges, steered round a bend and –

Where on earth were they?

They'd pulled up in front of a large modern
building at the end of the drive, a house of stone,
wood framing and acres of glass. Jamie had never
seen anything like it. There was a harshness about it,
but it was certainly magnificent in a sterile sort of
way. A smart-looking man was standing near the
front door talking to another man in Wellington
boots, overalls and holding a rake.

"What I wouldn't give to have a gardener," Max's
mum sighed as she pushed open the jeep door.

The smart-looking man finished his conversation
and strode towards them, smiling a welcome. Jamie
stared at him. He could feel the blood drain from his
face.

This wasn't any old smart-looking man. This was
his father.

3

No place like home

"Hi, Maggie, good to see you," said Mr Bryce, holding the jeep door while Max's mum slid down from the driver's seat.

"I hope this is really all right, Phil," she replied. "Richard needs the jeep tomorrow so it's easier to drop everything over now."

Philip Bryce glanced through the back window.

"I see you also have my son," he remarked.

Max's mum laughed. "We spotted him struggling up the hill. It seemed a bit mean not to give him a lift home as we were on our way here anyway. Max thought he ought to save his energy for the sleepover."

Jamie couldn't make sense of anything. What sleepover? And, yes, he had heard right. Max's mum had called this place "home".

Standing behind the jeep, she began to undo the straps holding the bike in place. Philip Bryce stepped forward to help her.

"Here, let me give you a hand. And *you*," he said, directing a hard look at Jamie, "where do you think you've been all this time?"

Jamie didn't know what to say.

"I...I didn't think you'd be home this early," he stammered. It was the truth.

"Well you thought wrong. Another time, you call me, understand?"

Jamie nodded. It was his dad's face, his dad's voice. But his manner? Jamie's dad had never been so sure of himself. He'd never had the confidence of this man. You could walk into a room and notice everyone in it, but completely miss Jamie's dad. You'd never miss the man standing beside them. There was something about him that leapt out and grabbed you by the throat.

Max began carrying the clutch of tents, sleeping bags and inflatable mattresses that his mum and Phil Bryce were hauling out of the back of the jeep to the front door.

"Come on, Jamie, lend a hand." Jamie's dad's voice wasn't one you'd readily disobey. He responded in a daze.

When everything was safely stowed in the big house's wide entrance lobby, through a fog of confusion, Jamie heard Max's mum mention something about quad bikes.

"Don't worry about the quads," his dad replied. "Jamie knows the rules, don't you?" and he flashed

Jamie a stern glance. "They wear helmets and they only use the bikes on the track over there, and then *only* if I'm watching."

Jamie had to concentrate very hard not to fall over.

Quad bikes? he thought. *Here?* Now I know I'm going nuts!

He watched as the jeep disappeared round the bend in the hedge-lined drive and out of sight.

"Hope you're a bit more awake tomorrow," Max called through the window.

But Jamie *was* awake. Wide awake.

"Right," announced his dad. "I'm just off to the station to pick up Leah. Chris is here, though," and he nodded his head towards the man in overalls who was now raking over the grass near where Phil Bryce had indicated the quad track. "You'll be all right?"

"Yeah." Jamie was still stunned. He hoped one word was enough.

He watched as his dad slipped into the driver's seat of a new silver Lexus parked in a bay just off the main drive and started the engine.

"Don't forget to put your bike away," Phil Bryce ordered as the car swept smoothly past him.

His bike. Jamie looked across to where the Stumpjumper was leaning against the house. So it wasn't a mistake. He hadn't somehow picked up the wrong one. It *was* his bike… And his dad drove a Lexus.

Left on his own, Jamie hoped Chris wouldn't come over and talk to him. He wanted to be by himself. He needed time to take in what had happened. How had he ended up in this crazy, unfamiliar world which, to everyone else, was apparently normal?

Put your bike away, his dad had said. That had to be his first job. From what he'd seen of him, Jamie didn't much like the idea of getting on the wrong side of Philip Bryce. He began to wheel it down the side of the house, and was vaguely aware of something else going on that he couldn't explain. He'd never been here before. As far as he was aware in his old life, this place didn't even exist. Yet his brain seemed to be telling him where to go, as if it was operating on some bizarre satellite navigation device.

There was a low, wooden building at the back of the house with a sloping, green-painted, corrugated iron roof. Jamie didn't hesitate, just pushed down on the door handle and wheeled the bike inside. He couldn't have known there would be a rack at the end where two other expensive-looking bikes were already standing, but somehow he did. He slid his bike in place then, without even thinking about it, crossed to the back door of the house and walked inside.

He found himself in a cloakroom. There was a row

of hooks on the wall, some of them supporting coats and macs and, at floor level, a double line of shoe lockers. Jamie went to kick off his trainers. To his surprise, he realised that these weren't the trainers he'd put on that morning, with the left upper coming away from the sole and the right lace knotted together where it had snapped several weeks before. These were new Nike trainers with barely a mark on them. Jamie examined them in disbelief. When did *they* get switched? Then, as if this was what he did every day, he pushed them into one of the lockers.

35

Through the cloakroom was a passageway with two doors, one to the side and the other at the far end. Jamie marched straight to the door at the end. He pushed it open and was immediately standing in a large kitchen opening onto an even bigger living-room space, with two huge, cream-coloured sofas, long, low, glass-topped coffee tables, a solid-looking sideboard and an impressive forty-two inch HD plasma television. He was seeing it for the first time, marvelling at the richness around him, yet at the same moment strangely familiar with these alien surroundings.

A broad, oak staircase swept up from the living-room to the first floor. Two corridors leading off a wide landing were punctuated by half-open doors. They revealed glimpses of tastefully furnished, comfortable bedrooms bathed in the light which poured in through vast panels of gleaming glass. Only one door was shut. Jamie ignored it and slipped into a room on the other side of the corridor. This was his bedroom. Somehow he just knew it. And it couldn't have been in greater contrast to his bedroom in Deal Street. Here, everything matched. Everything had its perfect place. There was a television, DVD player, laptop, stereo system, Playstation 3 – everything a boy could possibly want. Jamie took it all in in seconds, his mind churning so rapidly he thought his head would explode.

This can't be happening. It just can't be.

But it was.

He leant heavily against the bedroom door, snapping it shut, then felt himself slide down to the floor. None of this made any sense, but he was beginning to understand. He fished in his pocket and pulled out the leaf he had picked from the tree by the empty barn. He hadn't bothered to look at it at the time. The leaf was a deep, dark green, with six points and about the size of his hand. Despite being thrust into Jamie's warm pocket, it had lost none of its firmness or shine.

With a shudder of fear mingled with some kind of weird excitement and anticipation, all at once he knew for certain that the stranger he'd met wasn't mad. Jamie's obviously wealthy and high-flying businessman father, his big house on the far side of town, his pretend life – it was all here. By picking this one, mysterious leaf, Jamie had transformed his world. Completely. Everything was just as the man had said it would be.

Jamie was living his lie.

For a while he didn't move, just sat on the floor staring straight ahead blankly.

"We're back, Jamie."

His dad's voice calling up the stairs suddenly cut

into his thoughts. He started.

Back? he thought. Back from where? Oh, yes, back from the station. Phil Bryce had gone to pick up someone. Who was it? Jamie struggled to remember what he'd said.

Then his heart seemed to somersault.

Mum!

In Jamie's lie, his mum hadn't left. She still lived with them. With the shock of his arrival into this made-up life, he hadn't registered what his dad had said, but that's what he must have meant. He'd gone to pick up Jamie's mum! Jamie threw the leaf down onto his desk, flung the door open and shot downstairs.

A tall woman was standing in the kitchen with her back to him, filling a kettle with water. She had long, straight, blonde hair. Too blonde, Jamie thought afterwards. When she turned round, she glanced at him coldly with pale blue eyes set in a face which might have been quite pretty if it hadn't been hardened with too much make-up. His disappointment was overwhelming.

Without thinking, Jamie blurted out, "Who's this? Where's Mum?"

There was silence. Another pair of eyes were glowering at him darkly.

"What did you say?"

His dad's voice was soft, almost threatening. In a split second, Jamie realised he'd made a mistake. A big one.

"Sorry, Dad," he mumbled. He had a horrible feeling he was going to cry. "I didn't say anything. I think I've been asleep. I'm not feeling well."

"Oh dear," sighed the blonde woman without concern. "You'd better pop off to bed then, hadn't you?"

His dad reached out and touched Jamie's forehead.

"You don't feel hot. Leah's right, go and have a lie down. I'll call you when supper's ready."

As Jamie began to climb the stairs he looked back into the kitchen. His dad had slid an arm around Leah's skinny waist.

"Don't tell me he's got a bug," Jamie heard her whine. "The last thing I need is to go down with something else."

Phil Bryce shook his head. "No, don't worry," he said. "He's got his mates coming round for his big camping weekend, he's not going to miss that."

"Yeah," was the response, but Leah was unconvinced. "Well just keep them out of *my* way. This has been a hard week, I just want to relax."

"Not a problem," Jamie's dad replied soothingly, "it's all under control."

Then he kissed her. On the lips! Jamie couldn't

watch. He took the rest of the stairs two at a time.

Back in his room, his thoughts were once again hurling themselves around in his head. This wasn't how his lie went. His mum never left, that's what he pretended to his friends. She was away a lot, he'd told them, but she still lived with them, she still loved them. She still loved *him*. So why did his dad seem to have some blonde bimbo for a girlfriend?

Then it struck him – so hard it was like a brick slamming into his chest.

What if that woman wasn't his dad's girlfriend? What if she was his *wife*?

It was possible. In this weird, imagined life, if his mum had left, his rich, confident father could well have remarried, saddling Jamie with a fake blonde, over-made-up step-mum! He threw himself face down on the bed. What had gone wrong? In his head it had been a perfect lie. So where was his mum?

That's when a second brick smacked into him. Jamie sat bolt upright. For the first time since the start of this extraordinary adventure, he remembered his other dad, the quiet estate agent who'd swapped their one drab, grey life for another just as drab and grey. The dad at number 15 Deal Street may not have been everything Jamie wanted him to be, but at least he knew him. At least, in his own way, he was a dad doing his best for his son. Supposing that, locked away in some other world, this other dad was pacing up and down, looking at his watch, going repeatedly to the door, wondering what on earth had become of Jamie. Supposing he'd called in the police. They might even have a helicopter out.

Stop it! Jamie forced himself back to his new reality.

"My dad's downstairs," he said out loud, as though hearing the words would somehow help him to believe them. "He may not be anything like my dad but he is still my dad. This is what's real now. Freaky but, it might even turn out to be loads better than before. All I need to do is find Mum."

Supper later on with his dad and Leah was an uncomfortable experience. Jamie got the distinct impression that Leah would be far happier if he'd stayed in bed. At least it was useful for filling in the details of the weekend. Max, Callum, Megan and Abby were arriving tomorrow afternoon and they were all camping out in the garden for the night. Jamie's dad would make sure he was available between three and five o'clock so that they could go quad biking, and afterwards they could play around in the swimming pool while he lit up the barbecue.

So they did have a pool. Jamie almost wasn't surprised. It would explain Max's comment in the jeep about hoping the weather stayed good. Then they could spend the rest of the evening watching DVDs on the big screen in the games room, unless they'd rather play pool or table tennis. It sounded amazing. Jamie had to admit to himself that, for all his lies, he could never have made up anything so fantastic.

But there was a whole night to get through before then. He had to try and sleep. He wondered if it could still all turn out to be a dream. When he woke up, he might find himself back in his old, scruffy bedroom, with the smell of burning drifting upstairs as his nondescript dad overdid the toast. After all, it was a long time until morning.

Jamie didn't know how many hours he lay awake. Time dragged in the semi-darkness, but he must have drifted off because he woke much later with sunlight pouring in through the floor-to-ceiling windows of his new bedroom. It took him a moment to remember where he was – even *who* he was.

Then he realised. It was all still here. It hadn't gone away. Reality dawned. This was his life now.

4

Flying quad bike

In the kitchen, Philip Bryce was just finishing breakfast.

"Feeling better?" he asked as Jamie sat down.

For a moment Jamie didn't know what he meant. Then he remembered. He'd said he didn't feel well yesterday evening.

"Oh, yeah, thanks," he mumbled.

His dad stood up.

"Thought you might," he said meaningfully. "I've got some work to do this morning so I'll be in the office. We'll get the tents put up when the kids get here. They can all lend a hand."

He headed for the stairs, only turning back briefly to add, "And *don't* disturb Leah. She needs a rest. You'll all have to keep the noise down later."

And that was that.

Jamie sat on his own at the kitchen table staring after his father. He knew that every part of this extraordinary new life was going to take a huge amount of getting used to but, out of all of it, it was his dad who was going to take the most.

At about two o'clock that afternoon, Max, Callum, Megan and Abby piled out of the car that had pulled up at the front of the house. The twins' dad had brought them all over and he stayed long enough to help with the tents. Despite the chatter and excitement among his friends, Jamie couldn't help noticing that the two men didn't seem to have a lot to say to each other. The twins' dad was polite enough but reserved, and Jamie was left with the definite impression that he didn't like Philip Bryce very much.

An hour later, they were all lined up down at the quad track. There were two bikes out ready to take on the twisting circuit of curves, banking and humps that Jamie's dad had designed. Like everything else in this wealthy new world, the bikes looked brand new. They were Honda TRX 90s, black and red, with the distinctive wing logo emblazoned on the body. Other than Jamie, as only Callum had ridden a quad bike before, Jamie's dad had set the throttle limiters to a slow speed so that none of the children would be able to go too fast. Jamie was relieved that, in his old life, he had at least been on a quad once, and hoped this would be enough to make him seem less like a complete beginner.

He needn't have worried. Sitting astride the bike when it was his turn, most of his anxious expression hidden behind the blue and white full-face helmet, he was in complete control. Impossibly, as with all his new experiences of the past almost twenty-four hours, he knew exactly what he was doing. He even wished his dad would adjust the throttle limiter so that he could go faster. For the first time since his unexpected arrival, he began to think that maybe being here wouldn't be so bad after all.

It was Jamie's third turn. He was on the track with Abby who was getting more confident while Jamie's dad called out instructions. As he approached the banked curve at the far end of the track, he relaxed his thumb slightly on the throttle to slow down into the corner.

Something was wrong. Instead of losing speed, the quad began to accelerate.

Jamie let go of the thumb throttle completely, but still he went faster. He pulled back on the brakes hard. There was no response. Within seconds, he was hurtling into the steeply sloping bend.

Dad'll kill me! That was the first thought that burst into his head as he struggled to get control of the bike, remembering Philip Bryce's warning words yesterday – "Jamie knows the rules". He doubted whether tearing round the track at breakneck speed was listed anywhere in his dad's rulebook.

Then the impossible happened.

It was as though something had grabbed the bike's handlebars and wrenched the entire machine off the track. One hundred and ten kilograms of quad bike was suddenly soaring upwards as easily as if it weighed precisely nothing. Jamie tried to scream to his dad for help but the breath was sucked out of him as he felt the bike twist in the air. He could only cling on helplessly. Then, with a massive jolt, it landed on the other side of the hedge bordering the track, and sped away across the neighbouring field towards a huddle of trees at the bottom. Here, it came to such an abrupt halt that Jamie was thrown to the ground.

For a moment, he couldn't move. He lay there, stunned, waiting for the dreaded voice of his father yelling, "Jamie! What on earth do you think you're playing at?"

But there was silence.

Until – "That was quite a bump!"

It was a much quieter voice than the one he'd been expecting, and rather than anger, there was a trace of amusement. Jamie sat up sharply, aware of a pain in his right shoulder. He glanced round but he already knew who had spoken.

Peering down at him with eyes that seemed too small for his face was the stranger he had met at the old barn. A faint smirk was playing at the corners of his thin lips.

Jamie saw it and was angry. "I think I've wrecked my shoulder," he muttered, rubbing the sore joint.

"Yes," mused the man, "not a very smooth landing. Sorry about that."

But he clearly wasn't.

"Why are you here?" Jamie demanded, clambering stiffly to his feet. His whole body felt as if it had been thrown out of a first floor window.

"Just doing my job," replied the man casually. "A courtesy call. 'Checking in' I believe is the expression."

"Couldn't you have 'checked in' without breaking my shoulder?" Jamie complained.

He looked back towards his house. The quad had brought him quite some distance from the track, but there were still no outraged shouts, no concerned figures racing down the hill to find out what had happened to him.

"So tell me, Jamie," the man continued, "how's it all going? Is your lie everything you imagined?"

Everything he'd *imagined*? Jamie didn't know how to answer. He'd never really 'imagined' any of this. It was simply something he had made up to tell people, to give himself an identity he could cope with in front of them rather than letting them see what was real.

"I don't know," he found himself saying. "It's all so different."

"But is that bad?" the man asked, eyes twinkling. "You've got to admit it has a lot going for it. How many boys do you know with quad bikes at the bottom of their garden?"

Jamie couldn't argue with that. The camping weekend had got off to an amazing start.

"So relax!" cried the man triumphantly. "Enjoy yourself."

Jamie hesitated. "It's just that...I don't know if I'll ever get used to it."

"But you *must* get used to it, Jamie." The man's

tone was very direct. "After all, since you picked the leaf, you have very little choice."

Jamie frowned. "Yes I have!" he blurted out. "To get home I've got to tell the truth. That's what you told me." It wasn't much of a choice, but it was still a choice.

"Ah, yes," agreed the man, fingering his smooth, pointed chin, "I did say that, didn't I?"

He paused, eyebrows raised, then shook his head.

"Come on, Jamie, you and I both know that's not going to happen," he went on quietly. "Since when have liars been any good at telling the truth?"

Jamie stared. An uneasy feeling began to grip the pit of his stomach. Was he trapped here, then? Was there no way back?

"Stick with it!" the man continued. "You'll end up loving it."

"No!" Jamie was shaking his head wildly. "No! I can get back. You said if I'm not happy, I can get back! We had an agreement."

He searched the man's face earnestly, but the stranger merely sighed and took a couple of steps backwards.

"Oh, Jamie, you do surprise me," he said wistfully. "Agreements are based on honesty. And let's face it, there's nothing honest about our little deal. Is there?"

Then he vanished. In front of Jamie there was

nothing but empty space.

"Come back!" he screamed out. "Come back, we haven't finished!"

But there was silence and the air around him felt hollow. The stranger had obviously said everything he had to say.

Jamie felt his body sag. He thought he was going to fall over, but he suddenly became aware of the distant rumble of the single quad left on the track as it lumbered skilfully over the humps. Still no-one was shouting at him. No-one had come to find him. He managed to climb back onto his bike and was about to start it up, but it sprang into life on its own and swung round. Jamie clutched the handle bars tightly, his legs rigid. At least this time he knew what sort of a ride he was in for.

The quad took off back towards the house at dangerous speed and, at exactly the right moment, launched itself over the hedge. Jamie braced himself for the landing and just about managed to hang on. Then, as the wheels made contact with the track, the bike was suddenly back under his control.

He tweaked the throttle and headed steadily towards his father.

May as well get the shouting over with, he thought.

But there was none.

"All right, Jamie, off you get," his dad ordered. "Megan's turn now."

All right, Jamie, off you get? Was that it?

As Jamie got down and looked around, he gradually realised that there was no shouting because there was nothing to shout about. As far as his dad and his friends were concerned, his wheels had never left the track.

Messing about with his friends in the swimming pool an hour or so later was good for Jamie. He didn't have to talk much and it gave him the opportunity to thrash out some of his frustration. Part of him wanted to tell everyone the truth right now. Not even think about it, just do it. It was all the *thinking* that was driving him mad, all the questions chasing round and round inside his head. Would he ever get used to this new way of life? Was there really no way back to the old one? What would happen if he did tell the truth? And, the biggest question of all, how on earth had any of this happened? It was too much to deal with by himself, but who could he talk to? Only the stranger would take him seriously and Jamie was quietly hoping he'd never have to see him again. He'd rather talk to his toothbrush.

The hot, smoky smell of the barbecue filled the air. Jamie felt suddenly very tired. Exhausted. Much as he hated to agree with the man, he found himself having to admit that taking his advice might be best in the long run. Perhaps he *should* simply relax and enjoy himself. If he could only do that, maybe all the questions would go away.

As Jamie sat on a bench drying his feet, Leah brushed past him carrying a deep, wooden bowl brimming with salad. That was her contribution to the weekend. Jamie watched her put it down on the big oak table laid ready for them. She didn't speak, just exchanged a long-suffering smile with his dad then returned to the house.

That was another mystery. If this was supposed to be the lie Jamie had created, where was his mum?

In the games room that evening, he was still preoccupied. His friends were having a table tennis tournament and Jamie was meant to be keeping score but he couldn't concentrate.

"Oh, not again! I think Jamie's back in zombie mode."

Max grabbed a cushion and walloped him soundly round the head with it.

"What?" Jamie hadn't even realised they'd all been shouting at him.

"That was another game to us, deaf-ears!" Abby was beginning to get frustrated.

"So write it down because we're winning," added

Megan.

Max snatched the piece of paper Jamie was holding and looked at the scribbled scores.

"This isn't right," he moaned. "They've won four but we've won three not two."

"Sorry," Jamie muttered. "I've just got stuff on my mind."

"Yeah, I'll bet you have."

It was Callum who spoke. There was a sudden, awkward silence.

"What do you mean by that?" Jamie asked quietly.

"He doesn't mean anything," interrupted Megan, taking the piece of paper with the scores on from Max and thrusting it back into Jamie's hand. "Come on you lot, Abby and I've got a tournament to win."

Jamie shook his head. "No. I want to know what he meant."

For a moment no-one spoke.

Then Abby gave Callum a shove with her racket.

"Cal, you're such a loser. We agreed we wouldn't say anything."

"Say anything about what?" The back of Jamie's neck prickled. He had to know. Did they know about him? Had they been playing along, pretending everything was normal when all the time they knew he didn't belong, they knew he'd only stumbled on this rich kid's life by chance because he was a liar?

"Tell me!" Jamie's voice was urgent, almost angry.

"All right, keep your hair on," grinned Max. "It's nothing major. We just thought it'd be better if we didn't talk about the houses, that's all."

This was so far from the answer Jamie had been expecting that for a moment he was speechless.

"How long have you known about them anyway?" Max asked.

"Max!" Abby frowned.

"I'm only asking," he shrugged.

Jamie found his voice again. "What houses?"

To his surprise, the children all erupted into laughter. He looked at them blankly.

"What houses?" he repeated.

"Oh come on, Jamie, you can talk about it now," said Max. "It's hardly a secret anymore, the whole village knows."

Jamie shook his head. "I don't know what you're talking about."

"The development," chuckled Megan, not quite sure whether Jamie was messing about or not, "the new houses your dad's putting up in the village."

Jamie still looked lost so she added, "In the fields behind the park."

"My dad doesn't build houses, he just sells them."

Callum folded his arms disbelievingly. "How hard did Max hit you with that cushion?"

Jamie could feel himself getting annoyed. It was the same irritation he felt in his old life when people started asking too many questions. But, as he looked round at the four pairs of curious eyes fixed steadily on him, he realised that his friends knew all about something he *ought* to know all about. He had to think quickly if he was going to cover himself.

With an awkward smile he managed to say, "Had you going there for a minute, didn't I?" It was lame, he had to admit, but it was the best he could do.

"So you do know about the new houses?" Max said, not convinced.

"Of course I know about them," Jamie replied, "just not very much."

"Don't you ask?" pursued Callum.

"What for? I'm not really interested."

But, inside, Jamie was burning with curiosity. It had never occurred to him that his dad in his new life did anything different from his dad in his old life. It should have done, of course. His dad would never have got rich at that rundown little estate agents.

"Anyway," he remarked as breezily as he could, given that he was now desperate for information, "you seem to know a lot about these new houses already."

"We know there are going to be loads of them," said Abby. "Mum says your dad must be making a fortune."

"It's a good job you don't live in the village, though," Megan added.

"Why?" Jamie asked.

She gaped at him. "Do you have any idea how unpopular your dad is right now? Almost everyone's against what he's doing."

"Too right," agreed Callum. "I nearly wasn't allowed to come over this weekend. Dad was dead against it but then Mum said it wasn't your fault your dad's a property developer, so I got away with it."

"Well *I* think your dad's really clever," announced Max.

"How do you work that one out?" replied a disgruntled Callum.

"For saying he'll build the village a new school."

"What do you mean?" Jamie asked the question, then immediately wished he hadn't. He was obviously supposed to know about this too.

Max spoke to him as if he was talking to a dim-wit.

"Oh, come on, doughnut, keep up! He's going to knock down the old school and build a mind-blowing new one in exchange for being allowed to put up a load of new houses on some *really* nice fields that nobody wants built on – that's the deal your dad made with the Council. You and him really should talk more."

"*My* dad says it's evil," muttered Callum.

"Evil but brilliant!" Max replied.

"Still makes him public enemy number one in the village, though," said Abby.

"Well, almost." Max was grinning again. "Steedie loves him."

Mrs Steed was the Head Teacher of Wellbridge Primary. Her sallow complexion had recently acquired a satisfied glow from the knowledge that her school's facilities would soon easily beat most of the others in the area – and in time for the next OFSTED inspection.

So that was it. That was how Jamie's dad made his money, by getting his own way no matter what the cost. It was hardly likely to make him a hot favourite in the community, but perhaps Philip Bryce wasn't the sort of man to care what people thought about him.

Jamie felt a shiver run through him. He didn't want this – people steering clear of him, whispering about him in corners. He didn't want to be on the outside again. That was what he'd told all his lies to get away from.

"Right then, you lot. Grab your sleeping bags and get off to bed. You'd better try and get *some* sleep tonight."

Philip Bryce was standing in the gamesroom doorway. His expression was half-serious, half-smiling. Jamie didn't move, just looked at him. Who *was* this man? How could he be so different from the dad Jamie had left behind, the dad he wasn't sure he liked that much?

One thing he *was* sure of. He liked this one even less.

5

Sparks

It was Monday morning. Daylight was sifting between the cane blinds drawn down over the windows.

Jamie rolled over in bed and glanced at the clock. Half past five. Was that all? Still, he supposed he was lucky to have gone to sleep at all. He sighed and stretched out under the duvet. There was nothing synthetic about this one, of course. It was a goose feather quilt and the most luxurious thing Jamie had ever slept under. Draped across him, it felt downy and comforting, but it wasn't enough to take his mind off the unwelcome situation in which he'd landed himself. He'd been dreading this morning ever since his friends had gone home late yesterday afternoon. He felt fidgety and his body ached. He was exhausted.

Sleep had been in short supply camping out on Saturday night too. Megan had kept them all awake insisting she could hear strange noises outside her and Abby's tent.

"It's probably just an owl or something," Callum had suggested, trying not to appear bothered.

"It doesn't sound anything like an owl," had been

Megan's scathing reply.

"Then what *does* it sound like?"

"*I* don't know," she snapped. "Can't you hear it?"

"All I can hear is you wittering on," mumbled Max. "Isn't anyone going to sleep tonight?"

"How can I sleep when there's something outside my tent?" Megan whined.

Then she sucked in her breath sharply.

"What?" gasped Abby. "What is it?"

"Supposing...," she began, "supposing it's the Beast of Dartmoor!"

Max groaned. "But we're not *on* Dartmoor."

"It's not that far away," Megan persisted. "I mean, after all, foxes do it."

"Do what?"

"Go into towns at night. To raid dustbins and stuff."

There was an uncomfortable silence, broken finally when Abby piped up, "Are foxes anything to worry about?"

"Yeah," Max sniggered. "If you're a chicken. Can we go to sleep now?"

In spite of the restless night, Sunday had been a great day, a good part of it spent putting the Stumpjumper through its paces on the quad track. Philip Bryce's grand plans for Wellbridge hadn't been mentioned again and, just relaxing and messing about with his best friends, Jamie had begun to feel almost, well – normal.

But when everyone had gone home and he was left to his own thoughts, another question started to churn uneasily in his brain. What would life be like at school as Jamie Bryce, son of a wealthy property developer? And not just any old wealthy property developer, but one who, according to his friends, was in the process of making himself hugely unpopular.

No, Jamie hadn't expected to be able to get to sleep at all that Sunday night. Nor did he expect to drift off again with the early morning light already beginning to pour relentlessly into his bedroom.

It was the shrill pips of his alarm that forced his eyes open some time later, telling him it was half past seven. He fumbled for the switch and clicked it off. Then he groaned and buried his head in the duvet. Whatever had to be faced at school, this was the day he had to face it.

Less than an hour later, Jamie was steering his bike into the school car park. He was early. Mrs Steed's blue Honda Civic was already in its usual spot, but otherwise he was the first to arrive – which was exactly what he wanted. Being in school before everyone else and watching them gradually drift in sounded a lot better this morning than *being* watched ambling up the path just as the bell rang, which is what used to happen in his old life. In his old life, he would also leave his scruffy bike leaning casually against the railings bordering the car park. After all, who'd want to steal it? The Stumpjumper, however, he locked up carefully using the combination lock looped under his saddle. He wondered briefly how he could know the combination of a lock he'd never used. But it was like everything else he couldn't possibly know here. Somehow, he just did.

To Jamie's surprise, with the notable exception of Mrs Steed's cheery, "Good morning, Jamie" – which felt weird because she hardly seemed to notice him when he was the son of a small town estate agent, except to pass such comments as, "My goodness, Jamie, when was the last time your hair saw a comb?" – the school day passed much as he was used to. There was a lot of nattering with his friends about their camping weekend and when they might be able to do it again. In maths they did division; in literacy they were looking at *Treasure Island*; after break they did some research on the Roman Empire, and the art project in the afternoon on textures was still boring – just like last week. The only difference was that last week Jamie had been part of another existence. He'd gone into school that morning on the defensive only to find there was nothing to defend himself against. As far as he could make out, his

dad's scheme didn't seem to have upset anybody.
Perhaps nobody even cared. After all, he only had his
friends' word for it that the entire village of
Wellbridge was unhappy.

After school later in the evening, Jamie lay
stretched out on his bed trying to revise for a maths
test. Not easy, he realised, when you've just been
transplanted into a whole new life, and there's
enough going on in your head already without trying
to cram it full of maths as well. He'd had supper on
his own. His dad had been out at some meeting or
other and Leah had chosen not to eat with just Jamie.
Much to his relief. He couldn't imagine what they'd
have had to talk about.

Phil Bryce had come home a short while ago.
Jamie's enormous bedroom windows gave him a clear
view of the drive at the front of the house. He
watched as his dad slid the Lexus smoothly into the
parking bay, then climbed out, barely touching the
button on his key fob to flick the locks shut. He
always looked smug, Jamie decided, but this evening
he looked smugger still.

Jamie had just managed to drag his attention back
to the books in front of him for about the fiftieth time
when he heard another car outside. It roared down
the drive much too fast, then skidded to a halt on the
gravel close to the Lexus. Almost as if it was throwing

down a challenge, Jamie thought. Then the car door shot open and Callum's dad got out, slamming it behind him with tremendous force. His face was twisted with fury.

Jamie sat up. What was it? What could have happened?

Seconds later there was a frenzied hammering on the front door. Instinctively Jamie thought it must be to do with him. Something must have happened to Callum and somehow it was his fault! Why else would Callum's dad be here, pounding with his fists to be let in?

For a moment Jamie froze. Should he try and hide? Pointless! He knew his dad would find him anywhere. No. He'd just have to sit there and wait for the worst.

Only the worst wasn't at all what Jamie was expecting.

He heard his dad's voice shouting as he strode angrily to open the door.

"And just what do you think you're playing at?"

Before Philip Bryce could stop him, Callum's dad had brushed roughly past him, then turned to face him in the lobby.

"I might ask you the same thing!" he spat back, his teeth clenched.

"Get out of my house or I'll call the police." Bryce's

voice was lower this time but infinitely more dangerous.

In his bedroom, Jamie crept to the door and opened it a fraction. He could see Leah at the top of the stairs in a dressing-gown.

"What's going on, Phil?" she demanded.

"Nothing to worry about, sweetheart," he replied calmly. There was nothing in his tone now to suggest that he was anything but in complete control.

"Go back and enjoy your bath. Whatever Mr Renfrew wants to say he should have had the guts to say at the meeting this evening. Because now I don't want to hear it. So he was just leaving."

But Colin Renfrew didn't leave.

"You didn't give anyone a chance to say anything," he said grimly. "You've had this all wrapped up for weeks."

"So why are you bothering me now?" Philip Bryce asked. His disinterested tone was designed to send the sparks flying. And fly they did.

Callum's dad exploded.

"We trusted you!" he burst out. "Nobody wanted your grotty little houses, but we went along with it anyway. A development like this is just what the village needs, you said. It'll bring in new blood, you said. And as for that run-down school, out of the goodness of my heart I'll build you a brand new one, you said!"

"You're still getting your new school," Jamie heard his dad reply blandly.

"Yeah, but at what price, Phil?"

"The price of a few miserable hovels."

"Don't you call them hovels!" Colin Renfrew choked. "There are six, Phil. Six houses. Six *homes*. One of them's *my* home!"

"So what?" Bryce shrugged. "Six ugly blots on the village landscape. What are they worth compared to space for a school swimming pool? A proper sports hall? Believe me, they'll be so much more valuable when I've knocked them down."

Callum's dad was flabbergasted.

"It's where I live!" he spluttered. "It's where my family live!"

"You'll be re-housed. I've heard there's a nice little development going up at the end of the village."

Jamie couldn't see Colin Renfrew's eyes flash almost red with rage, but he heard the crash as he lunged wildly for his dad. Only he was smaller than Philip Bryce. Smaller and less agile. Bryce managed to side-step the attack neatly and, before Callum's dad knew what was happening, his arm was twisted behind his back and he found himself pinned face-first against the front door.

"Come on, Colin, you know I don't like violence."

His dad muttered the words so quietly Jamie barely heard them. Then he yanked Colin backwards, opened the front door with his free hand and shoved him out onto the driveway. Colin stared at him for a moment, breathing heavily. Then he shook his head.

"You won't get away with it, Phil. You'll never force us out."

Jamie could sense the smirk that must have spread across his dad's face.

"Sorry to disappoint you, Colin, but I'm afraid the choice isn't yours. You'll shortly be receiving a compulsory purchase order for your delightful little homestead. The Council's backing me all the way."

At the sound of the front door slamming shut, Jamie moved nearer the window and peered outside cautiously. Colin Renfrew looked white. Worse than white, almost transparent. He reached his car and leant heavily against it for a moment, as if he needed the support to stop himself falling over. Then suddenly, quite unexpectedly, just as he placed his hand on the driver's door handle, his head twisted round and Jamie found Colin Renfrew staring him full in the face. Horrified, he stumbled backwards out of sight.

But he'd already read the expression lurking in the man's dark, troubled eyes. What he saw there made him shudder. The blazing anger had been replaced with ice-cold hardness. And in the depths of his gaze skulked the shadow of pure hatred.

Jamie heard the car roar into life as it was started up and driven away at full pelt. Downstairs he was aware of his dad saying something to Leah. He couldn't catch the words, but there was an unmistakeable sneer in the laughter that followed.

He collapsed onto his bed. This new Mr Bryce may not be a man you'd miss in a crowd, but the old one would never have treated anyone so ruthlessly.

Sliding his leg across the bed, Jamie knocked his maths books onto the floor. It was pointless even to try looking at them again. Any hope he had of doing well in his test had just driven away with Colin Renfrew. If he'd been worried about going to school that morning it was nothing to how he felt about going in tomorrow. The future had been decided before he'd even arrived here. All the right bits of paper had been signed, the right hands had been shaken to clinch the deal. And now Callum, one of his best friends, was going to lose his home.

And not just Callum. Apart from all the occupants Jamie didn't know, Abby and Megan also lived in one of the six houses that made up School Row, at the far end. They loved it there.

How could he face his friends ever again after this? They'd never believe he didn't know anything about it. There'd be nothing he could say or do to convince them, he was certain of that.

Then Jamie had another sickening thought. It was no wonder his mum had left! If *he'd* been married to a man like Philip Bryce, he'd have left too. And nothing in the world would have persuaded him to come back, just as, he realised now, nothing in the world would persuade his mum to come back. Why couldn't she have taken him with her?

"Are you getting ready for bed, Jamie?" his dad called up the stairs.

"Yeah, in a minute."

But Jamie didn't move. He knew his dad wouldn't come in and see him. It would never occur to Philip Bryce to talk to his son about what had just happened. Whatever confronted him at school the next morning, he'd have to deal with it by himself.

Jamie locked up his bike against the railings. Whether he was early or late this morning, he couldn't see that it would make any difference. He'd still have to face his friends. So he'd opted for being late. The first bell had already gone and the playground was empty. But when he went into the cloakroom, it was obvious.

Silence fell.

Everyone knew.

Even Mrs Steed's greeting, as she breezed through on her way to the office, was more reserved than the day before. She must have known the extent of the building plans before yesterday only, now they were out in the open, perhaps she didn't want to be seen to be in league with the enemy.

That was what Jamie was now. If his dad was already public enemy number one, from now on so was he.

Then Jamie spotted him.

Callum. On the other side of the glass panel in the cloakroom door.

The second bell rang but nobody moved. Jamie waited for the door to be pushed open.

Suddenly they were all standing in front of him. Callum, Abby, Megan. And Max. Max wasn't going to lose his house but, from the expression on his face, Jamie knew he might as well have been.

"You knew, didn't you?"

As Callum spoke, all Jamie could see was that terrible look of hate in Colin Renfrew's eyes the night before.

"All that stuff at the weekend, pretending you didn't know anything about the new building. And all the time you knew your dad was going to knock down my house. Is that why you invited us all over? So you could have a good laugh at us for being too stupid not to realise you were up to something?"

"No!" Jamie shook his head miserably. "I didn't know!"

It was pointless to say it. Pointless even to think it. But what else could he do?

"How could you, Jamie?" demanded Abby quietly. "How could you not even tell us?"

"Because I didn't know. I didn't know about any of it, I promise!"

There was silence and all Jamie could do was squirm.

Suddenly the cloakroom door opened.

"Come along," said Mrs Steed briskly. "Bell's gone, you should be in class by now."

If she knew what was going on, she clearly wasn't going to say so.

The other remaining children, who'd hung around out of curiosity, shuffled past her as she stood holding the door open. Then, after a moment and without another word, Callum, Abby and Megan turned their backs on Jamie and walked away.

Only Max hesitated. For a second, Jamie thought he was going to tell him not to worry. Everything would be all right.

But he didn't.

Instead, in a low voice so that Mrs Steed wouldn't hear, Max muttered, "You're a liar, Jamie Bryce."

6

Desperate measures

It was almost half past four as Jamie slammed open the door of the green-roofed outbuilding behind the house where he stored his bike. When he'd gone to collect it from the school car park at the end of the day, there was no air in the tyres. Someone had pushed drawing pins into the rubber. It had taken him nearly an hour to wheel it home. He was hot and worn out. A headache had begun to clamp itself over his skull. Now he had to set to work changing tyre inner tubes. As if the day hadn't been miserable enough.

What had happened at school was devastating. If he wasn't being ignored or shoved out of the way, he was being whispered about. At lunch he was left to sit on his own. Someone even tripped him up outside the school hall. Jamie really had lost his friends.

The awful part was that he could only agree with them. He *was* a liar. His whole life here was a lie. A lie he'd made up to keep from happening the very thing that had now happened anyway, although this was worse than anything he could have imagined from admitting that his mum had left him. And even though, here and now, he was telling the truth when he said he knew nothing about his dad's plans – how could he when he'd only just arrived? – he knew it was useless. No-one would ever believe him.

Tears of helplessness and frustration began to prick at the backs of his eyes. For the first time in a long while, he wanted his dad. His other dad. His *real* dad.

He scrubbed off his hands in the downstairs cloakroom. The punctures were fixed but his head was still pounding. His new, power-hungry dad had popped out to see what he was up to, but apparently he was in the middle of something upstairs in his office, so he hadn't offered to help. He hadn't really seemed interested in how Jamie had managed to get two flat tyres at the same time.

As Jamie reached to turn off the tap, his phone vibrated in his pocket. He'd forgotten it was there. It made him jump.

There was a text from Max.

Can't have u round mine anymore.

Of course he couldn't. Jamie was amazed he was even bothering to text him. Maybe that was a good sign. He punched in a reply.

Really soz. Had no idea. Honest. Dad doesn't talk 2 me.

For a few moments the phone lay dead in his hand. Perhaps an answer was too much to expect. But finally it came.

No1 will ever trust u again.

Jamie's heart sank even further. Still, at least it was a response, even if it wasn't at all what he wanted to hear.

I know.

What else could he say?

He put the phone down on his desk and wandered across to the window. In the distance he could see Chris, the gardener, trimming back hedges that had begun to froth over with late spring foliage. Did that man ever go home?

The phone vibrated for a third time. Jamie was quick to snatch it up.

Got swim club 2night 6 – 7. Meet me in changing rooms after.

It took only seconds for him to tap back, *I'll be there.*

The swimming centre was only a short distance from Jamie's house, on the edge of town. It was part of a sports complex which, after a long overdue refurbishment had been smartened up considerably from its former tin hut-type feel. In his old life, Jamie had swum there frequently. Here, of course, there was a pool in his garden so he'd have no need to use it.

There were still twenty minutes to go before the end of Max's session as Jamie climbed the stairs to the viewing gallery, but he didn't want to be late.

"Got any homework?" his dad had quizzed when he'd asked if he could cycle down to watch Max swim.

And when Jamie had shaken his head he'd simply said, "Go on, then. Make sure you're back by eight."

As he'd ridden away, he knew Leah would be pleased he'd gone out. When he was at home he had very little to do with her, but she still seemed to resent his being there.

He leaned on the railing above the glass balustrade that bordered the length of the viewing gallery, watching. The swimmers were ploughing up and down the lanes, doing those flip turns at each end that he hated because of the water shooting up his nose.

Max spotted him but he didn't smile or wave. His mum was sitting at the far end of the gallery. Perhaps he didn't want to draw her attention to Jamie's presence. Or perhaps he'd dragged Jamie down here for the sheer pleasure of ignoring him. Then again, Jamie thought, he could just be concentrating on his front crawl. But he suddenly didn't feel comfortable where he was standing. He was too conspicuous. So he pushed open the double

doors and slipped back downstairs to wait for Max in
the changing rooms. They were empty when he
arrived and the recent improvements hadn't made
them smell any better.

He sat down on a bench round the back of the
lockers. It occurred to him that he hadn't stopped to
think why Max had asked him here. What was there
to say? Jamie had been as surprised by his dad's
plans as anybody, probably more so. But no-one
would ever believe that. Max was the best friend
Jamie had ever had and he'd called Jamie a liar.
What could they possibly have to talk about?

The changing room doors thudded back against
the rubber stops in the floor. They'd obviously been
carefully positioned to save the walls being damaged
as the red-painted wooden panels were hurled open
by young swimmers eager for the showers. Jamie
peered out from behind the lockers just long enough
for Max to see where he was. Then he slunk along the
bench back into his corner. As much as he didn't want
to be seen, he knew very well that Max didn't want to
be seen with him.

Max didn't bother to shower, but nor did he hurry
to get dried and changed. He was deliberately
hanging back, waiting for the changing rooms to start
to empty.

Eventually he slid along the bench to sit beside

Jamie.
He didn't
look at him.
He didn't speak
straight away either.
The silence between them was
awkward. Uncomfortable. It wasn't like sitting next
to Max at all, Jamie thought.

When his friend finally began to talk, if Jamie had
been expecting him to say anything, it certainly
wasn't this.

"You've got to talk to your dad. You've got to stop
him."

Jamie looked at him despairingly.

"How can I?" he murmured. "You've seen him. You
know what he's like. He's got it all sorted. All the
right people are obviously on his side. What can *I* do?"

"He's *your* dad, think of something."

Jamie could only shake his head.

"You don't understand."

Max looked at him. But there was no trace of the usual wicked grin that always managed to drag Jamie out of a bad mood.

"I understand you've betrayed your best friends," he hissed.

"But I didn't know what he was planning. I promise you, Max, I honestly didn't know."

"So you keep saying."

Max eyed him suspiciously for a moment. Then he stood up.

"I've got to go. Mum'll be waiting. Talk to him, Jamie. You're the only one who can. You've got to get him to change his mind. If you don't, never mind your quad bikes or your posh games room, you're not going to have any friends left to enjoy them with."

He paused. It was only the briefest of silences but it added a horrible weight to his final words.

"Not even me."

Then he picked up his bag and left.

Jamie sat gazing blankly at the empty wall in front of him. His head was still hurting. He leant it gently back against a locker. The changing room doors banged open again as two loud boys charged in shouting and laughing, ready for a swim. Jamie didn't move. They didn't know he was there.

All he could think was, how on earth can I talk to

a man like Philip Bryce? I don't even know who he is.

When Jamie got home, his dad was making coffee in
the kitchen. He could see Leah through in the sitting-
room stretched out on one of the enormous, cream-
coloured sofas watching television. Jamie had only
sat on it once. It was so soft it seemed to suck him
into itself like a huge marshmallow.

If he spoke to his dad now, Leah would overhear.
Perhaps it didn't matter. Jamie was as disinterested
in her as she appeared to be in him. But what was he
going to say? Whatever came out of his mouth it
wasn't likely to make any difference. From his
conversation with Colin Renfrew the previous
evening, it was clear that Jamie's dad was not a man
open to discussion. Least of all with an eleven-year-
old boy.

"Shut the door, Jamie. Don't hover."

As his dad spoke, the kettle clicked off. He picked
it up and tilted it towards the shiny cafetiere
standing on a tray next to it. In a moment he'd
wander through to Leah and Jamie would have lost
his chance. Such as it was. But he had to say
something. He couldn't face Max in the morning
without at least trying to change Philip Bryce's mind.

"Dad, can I talk to you?"

It was a start.

"Sure, for a minute. What is it?"

Jamie felt his heart leap into his throat. He couldn't stop now.

"It's all this new building."

His dad was reaching for the coffee mugs. He didn't look up.

"What about it?"

"Hardly anyone's talking to me," Jamie faltered. "My friends live in those houses. They think I've betrayed them."

He stopped, waiting for the response. Would his dad even understand betrayal?

Without even glancing at Jamie, he replied, "If they want to be small-minded enough to give you a hard time, that's up to them. They're all the same in this place. Frightened little ferrets who can't cope with a few changes. I've had to fight for this all the way. Don't let it get to you, you're better than that."

If that was meant to be a compliment, it was lost on Jamie. Philip Bryce picked up the tray, but Jamie hadn't finished.

"But they do have a point. I mean, it is where they live."

"They're going to get somewhere new to live."

"Maybe they don't want anywhere new," Jamie persisted. "Maybe they like it where they are."

His dad's eyes glinted and flicked towards him.

Jamie might hardly know this man, but he'd got a good idea of how far he could push him – and he reckoned he'd just reached the limit.

"In two or three years that village will be bending over backwards thanking me for what I've done. I've been here before, Jamie. I know what I'm good at."

Jamie felt suddenly irritated. This man was messing up people's lives. How could he be so smug?

The words were out of his mouth before he could stop them.

"Yeah. You're good at making money."

In a split second he saw the smugness on his dad's face turn hard. But Jamie was glad he'd said it.

"What I *make* is none of your business. Anyway, you do very well out of me."

Phil Bryce began to turn away.

"Dad, my friends hate me!" Jamie blurted out.

His dad threw him a fiery glare. What little patience he had had clearly run out.

"I'm losing interest in this conversation."

He paused.

Then, "Ride it out," he muttered. "In a few months it's not going to matter anyway."

Jamie frowned. What was that supposed to mean?

"Why not?"

"Use your head, Jamie. The place was only meant to be a stopgap. You won't be around to worry about it, will you?"

He walked away leaving Jamie standing in the kitchen, stunned. A stopgap? *Now* what was going on? Why wouldn't he be around? Were they moving away? No. His dad hadn't said "we" he'd said "you" – *Jamie* wouldn't be around to worry about it.

"Help yourself, sweetheart," he heard his dad say, indicating the coffee. "I'm just popping up to the office to make a phone call."

"Uh-huh," Leah nodded without taking her eyes from the television. If she was aware of anything going on between Jamie and his dad, she didn't even pretend to be interested. Jamie wondered whatever could have possessed him to marry a woman like that. Especially after being married to a woman like his mum. But then this Philip Bryce had probably driven his mum away.

Jamie slipped unnoticed up the stairs to his room. He glanced towards the office. The door was closed. He could picture his dad sitting comfortably at his desk, the phone pressed to his ear. He heard him laugh. Loudly. Harshly. What other lives was he plotting to turn upside down?

He kicked his own door shut and threw himself on the bed. His mind was racing. What had his dad meant? Where was he supposed to be in a few months' time if it wasn't here? How many more secrets was he going to uncover?

That's when it occurred to him.

Jamie was struggling to keep up with what was going on even though everyone assumed he already knew it all. If he could find out more then maybe he'd be able to get one step ahead. The more he knew about his dad's schemes, the better.

The office was there. Just down the corridor. He could sneak a look inside. He supposed there may be no information at all in the filing cabinets or the drawers of his dad's impressive oak desk, but it was worth a look. If they did hold a few nasty surprises, Jamie had to dig them out. And he couldn't hang around. With his dad working from home, there was no knowing when he'd next have the house to himself. Anyway, he wanted to have something to report back to Max the next day.

Jamie needed to do it when his dad and Leah were asleep.

Whatever happened, it had to be tonight.

7

Fabels

Philip and Leah Bryce were not the type to go to bed early. It was almost midnight. Each time Jamie went to his door to listen, he could still hear them talking or moving about. The glow from the lamps scattered around the sitting-room continued to drift up the stairs. Their bedroom was on the ground floor at the back of the house, with tall, heavily-curtained french windows opening onto the garden. If he crept into the office before they were asleep, Jamie probably wouldn't be heard, but it was still too risky. His dad was the sort of man to work well into the night, and until it was all quiet downstairs, there was no guarantee he wouldn't be back in his office, writing letters or, Jamie thought grimly, stirring up more trouble.

Jamie was exhausted. He had to force himself to stay awake. He tried to occupy himself by playing a game on the playstation (with the sound off so no-one realised he was still up), but in the end it wasn't enough to stop him drifting off.

It was just after half past two in the morning

when he woke. His head had rolled to one side as he slept and was lolling awkwardly over one of the padded arms of the swivel chair. His neck felt stiff and sore. The game he was playing was still up on the monitor but the controller had slipped from his grasp onto the floor. Jamie leaned forward to pick it up. Then he carefully slid the chair back into its place under the desk and switched the playstation off.

He opened the door a fraction and listened. Silence. More than that there was a stillness. The stillness of a sleeping house.

It took only a second for Jamie to snatch up his torch and creep out into the darkness of the landing. Outside the office, he stopped. No light glowed underneath the door. No sound emerged. The room was empty.

With his heart pounding in his ears, Jamie stepped inside Philip Bryce's office.

He closed the door gently. The catch clicked as he pushed on the handle. A sharp, metallic snap that echoed harshly through the darkness. Jamie froze. He didn't dare breathe.

In the rest of the house there was no sound. No movement. He'd got away with it.

Cautiously he flicked on the torch and swept the beam round. The room itself was sparsely furnished. Apart from the oak desk Jamie had glimpsed when the office door had been half-open one day – although this in itself took up a considerable amount of space – there were three four-drawer filing cabinets ranged along one wall, a black leather armchair in a corner opposite the window beside a square, wooden coffee table holding a neat pile of magazines, and a silver-grey, floor-standing reading light. On the desk itself, apart from the phone there was nothing. No mess. Nothing left lying around. Jamie doubted his dad even understood the concept of clutter.

He decided to try the filing cabinets first. He slid his fingers under the lipped handle of the drawers but with each one it was the same. Locked! That anything would be locked hadn't occurred to him. Why would his dad be locking stuff up in his own house? Didn't he trust them? Perhaps he was just worried about break-ins, but the alarm system Jamie had seen on the house looked powerful enough to alert an entire city police force, let alone the local station down the road. A burglar wouldn't stand a chance.

Jamie, on the other hand, was already inside. All he had to do was find the keys to the cabinets. He pulled on the handle of the top desk drawer. To his relief it opened. But there was nothing of any interest; stationery, stamps, paper clips, that sort of thing. Jamie rummaged through. There was no sign of a key. The next drawer down was no better, with just a folder full of what looked like household bills.

On top of two unopened packs of A4 paper in the bottom drawer was a glossy, expensively-produced brochure. Jamie shone the torch down and felt around for a key. He couldn't find one, but his attention was suddenly caught by the name on the brochure. It was a name he vaguely knew. There can't have been many people who hadn't at least heard of it: Fabels College. It was printed with a flourish in large, dark blue letters, and underneath in a smaller font were the words "Where education is for life".

The photograph on the cover showed a huge, elegant, red brick building set in immaculately landscaped grounds, with circular turrets rising above the roof and row upon row of magnificent windows. It was much more a castle than a school.

Jamie turned to the first page and read:

At Fabels, we pride ourselves on the quality of our staff and the education they deliver. Experts in their subjects, our teachers are lucky enough to work with pupils who not only benefit from their expertise, but also appreciate its value in their learning.

Why was this brochure sitting in his dad's drawer? Was he planning to demolish this school as well? As Jamie flipped through the pages, a letter fell out. He picked it up and shone the torch onto the stiff, dusky blue paper. The letter was addressed to Philip Bryce – from Fabels College.

Dear Mr Bryce,

Many thanks for your letter regarding your attendance at the Parents' Reception Lunch on 8th September. We are sorry that you will be away on business at that time and therefore unable to attend. However, we look forward to welcoming your son, James, on that day as he begins boarding with us here at Fabels.

Yours sincerely,
M. J. White
Personal Assistant to Mr Pope, Principal, Fabels College

Boarding with us?

Horrified, Jamie looked at the date on the letter. 28 April – only last month. And the address on the notepaper told him the school was in Hampshire. Hampshire! That was miles away!

So that's what his dad had meant. Jamie wouldn't be around to worry about what was going on at Wellbridge Primary because he was being sent away to boarding school. And, as with everything else in this weird new life, this wasn't just any ordinary boarding school. It was probably one of the most

expensive in the country. How had that happened?
How had he got in to a college like that? Had he been
to an interview? Had he taken an exam? Or perhaps
his dad had just bought their way in the same as he
seemed to do with everything.

That was when Jamie heard the click.
Instantaneously the office was flooded with a harsh
brightness as the light was snapped on. He jerked his
head up, dropping the torch and the brochure and
stood, blinking helplessly in the unforgiving glare.

"I hope you've got a good explanation for this."

As he stood in the doorway, Philip Bryce's voice
was quiet, menacing.

Jamie was paralysed.
He'd been so staggered
by the letter he hadn't
noticed the office door
swing open. He didn't

seem to be able to take in a breath.

"I couldn't sleep," he managed to gulp finally.

"It doesn't look as if you've been to bed."

What an idiot! Jamie thought. He wasn't even in his pyjamas. Why hadn't he got undressed? Then at least he could have pretended he was sleepwalking or something.

"I'm waiting, Jamie."

Jamie could feel a lump rising in his throat. For the first time since the start of this bizarre adventure, he was really frightened. He was trapped in a lie that he didn't want but, even so, it should have been perfect. So why had it all gone wrong? He had no mum. He'd lost his friends and in a few months he was going to be shipped off to boarding school – that had to be Leah's idea – so he wouldn't even have a proper home. Not that this was anything like home.

Desperately, he tried to swallow back the panic.

"I didn't go to bed. I wasn't tired. There's been so much going on. I was on a game but..."

Jamie broke off and his gaze travelled to the floor. Fabels College was staring back at him blandly from the glossy photograph. It gave him a way out and he grabbed it.

"I couldn't stop thinking about my new school," he faltered. "I just wanted to look at the brochure... again. That's all. I thought there'd be one in here."

He could feel his dad's eyes boring into him. He daredn't look up.

"It's three o'clock in the morning, Jamie."

"I know. I'm sorry."

There was a pause. His dad looked down at the brochure lying at Jamie's feet. Slivers of plastic lay beside it. The torch had smashed as it hit the floor.

"Why didn't you just turn on the light?" he quizzed.

"I thought I might wake you," Jamie answered. It was the truth. "I thought you might think we had burglars or something."

"Oh, I did."

His dad considered him for what seemed a very long time. Would Jamie get away with it? Would he be believed? When Philip Bryce eventually spoke, Jamie still couldn't be sure what was going on inside his head.

"Go back to your room and go to bed this time. You're old enough now, I shouldn't be having to run checks on you. Take the brochure. But you look at it tomorrow, not now. You understand?"

Jamie nodded. He bent down to pick it up, with the battered remains of his torch, and headed for the door. But his dad was still blocking the way. There was a moment's uncomfortable pause before he stood aside to let him past.

As Jamie drew level with his bedroom door, his dad's voice stopped him again.

"One more thing."

Jamie slowed and, very unwillingly, glanced back at him.

"I don't ever expect to find you in here again. Is that clear?"

"Yes, Dad." It was about all Jamie could mumble. "Sorry."

He managed to push open the door and slink gratefully into his bedroom. But he didn't turn on the light. Once he was safely shut in, the darkness seemed to overwhelm him. Powerless to stop them, his legs buckled. He hit the floor and the tears he'd been holding back began to spill down his face.

As he lay curled up in the dark, there was one thing he was absolutely sure of. He couldn't live with this any more.

He had to get home.

8

Liar

When Jamie opened his eyes, it was daylight. He must have fallen asleep crumpled on his bedroom floor. He woke feeling stiff and bruised. His head ached viciously and there was a sick feeling in his stomach.

But Jamie had made up his mind.

If his only way back home was to tell his friends the truth, then that's what he would do. After all, they already hated him. How much worse could it get?

Still there was one huge problem. If they thought he was a liar, would he ever get them to believe him? And, according to the stranger whose words had led him here to begin with, if they didn't, he was stuck with his lie forever. Worse still, so were they.

Then it hit him. The second big problem.

The stranger up at the old barn had said that, if he wanted to go back to his other life, he had to make his friends believe what he told them before the end of seven days. It was already Wednesday. He only had until Friday after school to sort things out and get home. Barely three whole days. Beyond that...

No. Jamie couldn't even bring himself to think about it.

In the kitchen, his dad was looking through post, a mug of tea steaming on the table in front of him. He didn't look up. Jamie crossed to the back door.

"I'm off to school," he mumbled, turning briefly as he reached for the handle.

"Not having breakfast?" His dad still didn't look at him.

Jamie shook his head. "No, I'm not hungry."

"Must be all that creeping about."

Jamie waited for the eye contact but it didn't come. His dad simply picked up another envelope and slid his thumb under the flap to open it. Perhaps that would be it. The only reference to last night that Philip Bryce would make. Jamie slipped out and went to fetch his bike.

School was just as bad as the day before. Worse, really. He'd cycled in with the hope that at least Max might be a tiny bit on his side. But when Jamie tried to talk to him at morning break, he walked away. He didn't want to be seen with him. How could Jamie tell him what had happened last night if all he did was turn his back?

At lunch, Jamie had his name ticked off on the register, but he didn't join the queue. He was hungry.

He hadn't had breakfast. Still he'd rather starve than sit on his own in a corner. Any other time he'd have pretended to be ill and tried to get sent home but, apart from school, home was the last place he wanted to be. He thought about just walking out, cycling up to the old barn and spending the afternoon there, but if he did that, not only would he be in even more trouble, he'd also lose any chance of talking to Max before the end of the day. And somehow he *had* to speak to him. He had to get him to listen.

It was a split second decision. Crazy, really, because if he was discovered he'd probably get sent home anyway. But the corridor was empty and he needed space to think, somewhere he could work out a plan. Tentatively he pushed on the door of the staff cloakroom and peered in. As far as he could tell, it was empty. Teachers obviously didn't hang around in the toilets the way the pupils did.

It took only a moment to whip into one of the cubicles and lock himself in. In the boys' toilets, he'd be discovered. Anyone spending longer than two minutes behind a locked door was hounded until they came out. In here, a teacher would just assume he was another teacher. At least that's what Jamie hoped.

He'd hardly sat down when he was aware that something curious was happening to the cubicle door.

It didn't look solid. As he watched with widening eyes, it began to bulge towards him as if it was made from some sort of peculiar rubber. Jamie leapt up. At the rate the door was swelling inwards, it would only be moments before he was sandwiched between the bulge and the back wall of the cubicle. He'd be crushed! There wouldn't even be time for him to crawl under the partition into the next toilet. He wanted to cry out but the breath seemed paralysed in his lungs.

Jamie tried to flatten himself into the cubicle corner. He squeezed his eyes closed.

Suddenly, the door snapped back.

"Dear me, Jamie. I didn't think you were the type to hide in the toilets."

He knew before he opened his eyes. Standing in front of him, adjusting his jacket, was the stranger.

"Did you just...walk through that door?" Jamie was incredulous, but the man was dismissive.

"Just a little trick I learned. You'd be surprised how not useful it is, actually."

Jamie was beginning to think that nothing would surprise him ever again. What could be more absurd than being jammed in a staff toilet with a man who'd just walked literally *through* the door? Yet here he was.

"Well, I must say," continued the stranger, "I'm very surprised to find you're still so miserable."

That was too much for Jamie. Something inside him exploded.

With difficulty he kept his voice low as he blurted out, "What did you expect? You want to know why I'm miserable? Because of you! Because you put me here! I hate it! I want to go home!"

"Oh Jamie," the man sighed. "I'm not the one who put you here. You did that all by yourself – the moment you chose to be a liar."

"I didn't 'choose' anything," Jamie hissed. "'Pick a leaf,' you said. *I* didn't know what I was doing."

"But it was your lies that led you to the Lying Tree. Not me."

"No." Jamie shook his head. "You tricked me."

The man shrugged. "Now you and I both know that's not true. You had a choice. You chose your lie."

"Well now I'm un-choosing it."

"Why? This is the life you told your friends about. This is what you wanted everyone to believe."

Jamie could feel himself floundering.

"But it was never meant to be real," he argued. "I didn't *want* any of it. I just didn't want anyone to know…"

His voice trailed off.

"To know what?" the man asked. "The truth?"

Jamie nodded miserably.

There was a pause. Then he burst out, "I can't stay here. I've lost all my friends. I'm being packed off to boarding school. My dad's some sort of power freak. And where's my mum? I used to pretend she'd never left but she'd never stick around someone like him. He's all wrong. He's just not like my dad."

The stranger raised his eyebrows.

"But your other dad wasn't good enough, was he? You couldn't tell people he was just an ordinary estate agent. That wouldn't have been nearly so interesting. Can you see your other dad as a successful, high-powered businessman? I don't think so. He could never have done what this man's done."

He stopped and fingered his buttons thoughtfully.

"And as for your mum, that's the part of your lie you never really believed in, isn't it? You could say the words, but in your heart you could never even begin to imagine what life would have been like if she'd stayed. Sad really I suppose, but that's why she's still gone."

That was it, then. If Jamie had already decided to

try and get home, now he was even more determined. There was nothing for him here. Not even hope.

Gulping down the sobs that were once more threatening in the back of his throat, he said, "That's why I'm going, too."

The stranger was silent for a moment.

"So, you're proposing to do what?" he asked at last. "Tell the truth?"

"Yeah," Jamie nodded, "that's exactly what I'm going to do."

The sound of the cloakroom door swinging open interrupted them. Footsteps tapped their way into the next cubicle. Jamie watched the man, imploring him silently, "Please don't do the door thing again. No-one can know I'm in here."

The man's pale lips formed themselves into a thin, cold smile. He leaned forward, bringing his mouth level with Jamie's right ear.

"Well, I wish you luck. The agreement was for seven days. You only have until Friday at..."

He stopped and glanced at his watch.

"Ah yes. Five o'clock. Time's running out. And let's face it, Jamie, who's going to believe a liar like you?"

Then he vanished. Through the door, into thin air, Jamie had no idea. But he was gone. Jamie couldn't even shout out after him. He couldn't risk being discovered.

Outside in the corridor, the bell rang. Now he had to get out of here without being spotted. He heard the cloakroom door open again and the lock on the third cubicle snap shut. If he waited, someone else would come in and he'd be stuck there even longer. He needed to go now. He had to try and corner Max before lessons started again.

Cautiously, Jamie slid back the bolt and stepped out of his cubicle. But when he reached the cloakroom door, it began to open towards him. All he could do was dive behind it. Mrs Steed didn't spot him. As it swung closed, revealing his hiding place, she was already locking herself in the cubicle he had just vacated. Unseen, he peered out into the corridor. Three class 2s were standing talking with their backs to him. There was no-one else.

He was out.

When he walked into the classroom, a hush descended. Thirty pairs of eyes followed him as he sat down.

"Don't stop talking on my account," he muttered.

At the corner table, Max was carefully avoiding looking at him. Jamie would never be able to talk to him. Not here.

The teacher walked in as he was scribbling a note: *Max I've got to talk to you. Meet me after school. It can be anywhere you want. Just _please_ meet me. Jamie.*

Later in the afternoon when Jamie had to go and get a book, he sidled past Max and dropped the note in his lap.

It wasn't until the end of the day that Max responded. In the cloakroom, he brushed past Jamie who felt him push something into his pocket. Jamie waited until he was outside by his bike before fishing it out. On a scrap of paper Max had written: *Meet you at church bench. 4.30.*

4.30! That left Jamie an hour of hanging around. Perhaps that was the idea. After all, why should Max make things easy for him?

He remembered to text his dad.

Seeing Max after school. Back by 6.00.

Hopefully there wouldn't be any questions and he'd just assume Jamie had made it up with his friends.

The church bench was a wooden seat whose four legs rested squarely on each of the four small bricks set into the grass behind the church. It carried a brass memorial plaque engraved with the words *IN MEMORY OF MOLLIE RATCLIFFE, POSTMISTRESS IN THIS VILLAGE FOR 48 YEARS*. Jamie had read it before. All around him, everything in his new life was exactly as it was in the old one. With the exception of his own existence, which had changed beyond all recognition. The bench was an odd meeting place, but Jamie understood why Max had chosen it. It was quiet. Private. People passed through quickly more than hung around. They were less likely to be noticed.

Jamie stretched out on his back on the seat and closed his eyes. His head wasn't just aching, it felt strange, but then he hadn't eaten all day. For now he'd got more important things on his mind than food. Telling the truth was only part of the answer. He'd have his work cut out trying to get Max to believe him.

He woke with a start. Max had shoved his feet roughly off the end of the bench and plonked himself down in their place.

"I haven't got long," he muttered. He wasn't looking at Jamie. He was keeping an eye on the gate at the far end of the churchyard in case anyone should come in.

"Neither have I," Jamie answered. "Nor have any of us if we're going to get out of this mess."

"I already told you," Max huffed indignantly, "*you're* the one who's got to sort it out, not us. If you've got nothing new to say…"

"I *can* sort it out. Just not in the way you think." Jamie hesitated. "And I can't do it on my own."

Max glanced at him scornfully.

"You don't seriously expect me to help you?"

No. What Jamie needed Max to do was believe him.

He started to try and explain what had happened. Without his best friend on his side, he knew he could forget about ever getting home. Max would probably think he was nuts but what choice did he have? In some ways it would be a relief. For the first time in a long while, he could stop pretending.

To Jamie's surprise, it was amazingly easy. The words poured out. He told Max how his mum had left him and his dad, so they'd moved here to try and make a fresh start. He'd started to lie about everything because he was ashamed, because at his old school he'd been teased and laughed at. He'd wanted people here to think he was somebody different. Not the kind of boy whose mum left because she couldn't see the point in staying. He hadn't meant to hurt his friends, he just didn't want them to know who he really was.

Only it had all gone wrong. The lies had got out of control. He didn't know how to keep them all going.

Then – and this was where it got harder to explain, because no-one in their right mind would believe it – he started to talk about the strange man he'd met and how, by picking a leaf from some tree that shouldn't even have been there, he'd ended up here. If he could only get back to his other life, everything would be back the way it was because, in his other life, none of this was happening. His dad wasn't a property developer about to knock down his friends' houses. He was a harmless estate agent. And not a very good one, either.

Max listened in silence.

"Is that it?" he asked finally. He was staring down at his shoes.

"That's it. That's the truth."

"You're such a liar."

Jamie shook his head.

"No! I mean, yes, I *am* a liar, but I'm trying not to be. I'm trying to tell you what's really going on. The trouble is, just telling you isn't enough. If things are going to get back the way they were, you've got to believe me."

Max stood up. He'd had enough.

"I thought you were going to tell me you'd spoken to your dad. Instead you just give me another load of lies. How long did it take you to think that lot up? You must have been awake all night."

"I *was* awake all night!" Jamie could feel the desperation building inside him. If he lost Max now, he'd never get him back.

"I *tried* to talk to Dad. I even went through the stuff in his office to try and find out more about what he's going to do. He caught me. I thought I was dead."

"You're an idiot, Jamie," was Max's only response. "I've got to get home."

Jamie leapt up and stood in front of him, blocking his way.

"No, please, you've got to listen to me. I know I've messed up. I know I shouldn't have lied but I swear *this* is the truth. There's no reason why you should believe me, I know, but think about it, Max. If you *do* believe me, you've lost nothing. But if you don't, you could lose everything! We all could."

Max stared at him.

"Wrong," he answered. "If I say I'll believe you, I could lose my friends. Just like you have."

Then he shook his head and pushed on past.

"We've only got until Friday, Max!" Jamie shouted after him. "Friday, five o'clock. If you don't believe me by then – all of you, that's you, Cal, Abby and Megan – we're stuck with this for ever."

The gate at the top of the path swung back. Max was gone.

All evening, Jamie waited for a phone call. A text. Anything. But there was nothing.

As he lay on his bed, the stranger's cold little smile danced in front of his eyes and his parting words echoed round and round in his head. It was hopeless.

Let's face it, Jamie. Who's going to believe a liar like you?

9

Dead end

Max did send a text that evening but it wasn't to Jamie. He texted Callum to see if they could meet up later with Abby and Megan.

They all sat round in Callum's bedroom listening gloomily as Max told them everything Jamie had said. When he'd finished, no-one seemed to know quite what to say.

Finally Callum scoffed, "You sound as if you believe him."

"I don't know what I believe," Max snapped. "I mean, it's a load of rubbish, isn't it? I just don't know why he'd say stuff like that."

"Because he's a liar," replied Callum grimly. "It's what he does."

"Well, we know one thing, Max," Abby announced. "He doesn't care how he gets your friendship back. He's just trying to get you on his side. He's trying to make you think, 'Oh poor Jamie, he's had such a hard time'."

"Which doesn't change the fact that he's been lying to us," added Megan.

"*Has* he though?" Max was looking more and more doubtful.

"He told you he has, himself."

"Yeah, but what's he been lying about?" Max persisted. "He still says he didn't know anything about all this building stuff. He says he lied to us about his mum and dad, and having loads of money."

"Max," Megan said disparagingly, "we *know* he's got lots of money. We've been to his house."

"Exactly!" Max exploded. "So why admit to lying about something that can't possibly be a lie? He didn't have to do that. He didn't have to say he was a liar at all."

He paused. The more he thought about it all, the more confused he felt.

"Look," he went on more quietly, "if Jamie says he didn't know about your houses being knocked down then maybe in the end we just have to accept that. There's no reason why his dad should have told him, especially if he was trying to keep the whole thing a secret. Why risk it? But the rest of it…"

He stopped again and looked round at his friends.

"It's not going to make us think any better of him, is it? The opposite, really. He's saying he's been lying to us since he's known us. Why go to the trouble of telling me all that – unless it's the truth?"

There was silence.

"He's obviously a loony?" Megan suggested.

Callum ignored her and scowled, "So, what are you saying, that what's happening isn't real? It's all just some figment of Jamie's imagination?"

"I don't *know*." Max shrugged helplessly. "It's just that…whether what he said was true or not, I don't know why but I honestly think he believed it."

Abby folded her arms. "Now you're just being stupid."

"No, I'm not. Think about it. Jamie was acting really weird last weekend. He didn't seem to know what was going on. And when we gave him a lift home on Friday after school, you should have seen his face. We stopped outside his house and it was as if…as if he'd never been there before."

Callum's eyes narrowed.

"So you've come round here because you want us to believe him?" he frowned.

"But, don't you see," replied Max, "if Jamie's not making this up then this whole situation isn't real. The new houses, the new school, you having your houses knocked down. Us here now isn't real! If going along with him can get things back to normal, isn't it worth a try? If it doesn't work we're no worse off. At least we'd know for certain that Jamie's just a liar."

There was a moment's pause.

Then, "You're nuts!"

Callum was angrier than the others. His dad and Philip Bryce were deadly enemies. From now on, so were he and Jamie.

"If you want to listen to Jamie Bryce," he hissed, "that's up to you. But don't drag me into it."

"Jamie said it had to be all of us, Cal," Max said slowly. "We've *all* got to believe him. If you're not going to then…we'll never know if he's telling the truth or not. This'll be what we're stuck with."

Callum gave him a moody kick.

"*You're* not stuck with anything," he muttered. "It's not *you* who's losing his house."

When Jamie woke on Thursday morning, it was wet and miserable. Rain was deluging down outside. He went to put on his waterproofs in the utility room but his dad stopped him.

"You can't cycle in weather like this. It's desperate out there. Hang on for five minutes and I'll take you."

"No." It was the last thing Jamie wanted. "I'll be fine."

"I'll take you, Jamie, just wait. I've got to pop out anyway."

His dad was insistent. Jamie would rather have got soaked to the skin than be trapped in a car with Philip Bryce for fifteen minutes, but he could see he had no choice. They both sat in silence as the Lexus glided effortlessly down the drive, wipers swishing away the rain that ran in rivulets down the slope of the windscreen, and turned left onto the main road.

At the top of the narrow lane leading down the hill into Wellbridge, they came face to face with a large, blue van. There wasn't room for two vehicles to pass each other here. They just stopped dead, bumper to bumper.

Jamie's stomach hit the floor.

It was Colin Renfrew.

The two drivers sat staring at each other.

"Don't you think you ought to back up?" Jamie asked hesitantly. He didn't want any more trouble.

"I'm not backing up for him," his dad murmured in response, his eyes fixed steadily on the other man. Colin Renfrew clearly had no intention of backing up either. Jamie wished someone else would come along, but they were on their own.

Finally the door of the blue van swung open. Ignoring the driving rain, Callum's dad marched up to the Lexus driver's window and banged on it forcefully. Jamie went cold.

"Back up, Bryce." The words were spat more than spoken. "Just because you own the village doesn't mean you own the road as well."

Philip Bryce ignored the assault on his window and continued to stare straight ahead of him. Colin pointed angrily up the hill.

"Back up into that gateway now!" he shouted. "Or shall I just ram you?"

"I'd like to see you try," Jamie's dad responded too quietly for Colin to hear.

"Dad..." Jamie began. But his dad wasn't listening. Very deliberately, he leaned forward and switched on the radio, turning it up to full volume. Jamie winced.

Thumping with all his might on the window, Callum's dad yelled out, "Get out of the car, Bryce! Let's sort this out once and for all!"

Jamie wouldn't have been surprised if the force of the pounding released the airbags. A chill sweat began to prickle all over his body.

Then suddenly Colin stopped. He twisted his head to look back up the hill. Another car was slowing and drawing up behind the Lexus.

"You'd better start looking over your shoulder, Bryce," he hissed through clenched teeth, his mouth almost touching the window. "You can bully the rest of the world but you can't bully me. One way or another, I *will* get you."

He jabbed a bitter finger into the glass and, with that, had no choice but to return to his van and reverse back down to the bottom of the hill.

Jamie was trembling but his dad didn't notice. He

was too busy smirking at the retreating figure of Colin Renfrew.

He reached forward and clicked off the radio, then murmured softly, "Not if I get you first."

And Philip Bryce wasn't the kind of man to make empty threats.

Jamie got out of the car outside school and picked up his bag from the back seat.

"Got money for the bus home?" was all his dad asked.

Jamie nodded. He didn't know whether he had or not, he just wanted to get away and preferably without being seen getting out of his dad's car.

He was about to cross the road when his dad called to him. What now?

"Stay away from Callum Renfrew." Philip Bryce's voice was flat. Disinterested. "That whole family's a waste of space."

Max and the twins were already in the classroom when Jamie walked in. They pretended not to see him but he took no notice and marched straight up to them. There wasn't enough time left to play games.

"Can I talk to you, Max?" It was more a statement of intent than a question.

"Anything you've got to say you can say in front of us," said Abby. "Max has told us what you've been telling him."

"And?" Jamie glared at her.

"And nothing," Abby shrugged. "You can't *make* us believe you."

Jamie wasn't going to be put off.

"Every day we're here, things are getting worse and worse. I may be a liar but I could never have thought all *this* up. I'm not that clever."

"You're right there," Max remarked dryly. As Jamie looked at him, he caught almost the hint of a twinkle in his pale blue eyes. And he grabbed onto it.

"Please, Max."

The second bell rang and Callum wandered into the classroom. As he pushed back his rain-soaked hair, he spotted Jamie with the others. A look of disgust crossed his face and he went and sat on his own on the other side of the room. Max watched him thoughtfully for a moment.

"I'm not saying we believe you because we don't," he said. "But if you are telling the truth, it's not really us who need persuading."

With that, he cast a meaningful glance at Callum and walked away with the twins.

If you're telling the truth? That's what Max had just said. It wasn't much but it was enough to give Jamie a glimmer of hope. If he could only win Max over today, then the two of them could work on the twins, which might still give him time to persuade

Callum before five o'clock tomorrow afternoon. It wasn't long. But Jamie knew that, somehow, it had to be long enough.

The rain didn't let up at morning break or at lunchtime, so no-one was allowed outside. There never seemed to be a moment when Callum was on his own, and whenever Jamie tried to get near him, he walked away.

At the end of the afternoon, he had one last try. But Callum had had enough. He spun round and pushed Jamie back against the wall.

"Just stop bugging me, rich boy," he snarled. "You may think you can lie your way out of everything, but you can't. You're such a loser."

The worst of it was, Jamie could only agree with him. His rucksack slung over one shoulder – he'd found some change in the bottom, enough for his bus fare home – he walked gloomily down the path towards the school gates. The heavy rain had slowed to a fine, irritating drizzle. If he walked quickly he'd be able to get to the stop at the end of the village before the bus arrived. He didn't want to hang around at the shelter outside school. At that precise moment, if he could have found a suitably sized hole in the ground, he would quite happily have crawled into it and stayed there.

He started down the steps by the changing huts.

Whether or not he was aware of the door being whipped open, he couldn't be sure. It all happened so quickly. But, without warning, he was almost yanked off his feet. Someone had grabbed his arm and pulled him roughly into the girls' changing room, slamming the door shut behind him.

He saw Megan first, sitting on a bench in front of him, arms folded. Then he was jerked sideways onto the bench opposite. Only now did Abby let go of his arm as she plonked herself down next to him.

Megan was looking him squarely in the face.

"Right, Jamie, you're going to tell us the truth."

Jamie rubbed his arm. Abby had grasped it in a surprisingly vice-like grip and it really hurt. She didn't look that strong.

"We're waiting," Megan snapped.

"If you listened to what Max told you," Jamie muttered dismally, "you already know the truth. Anyway, you all think I'm lying so what's the point in going over it again?"

"The point is we want to hear it from *you*."

Jamie shook his head. "I'm going to miss my bus."

"Tough," said Abby flatly. "You want us to believe you, don't you? So just tell us, Jamie! What's going on?"

To his annoyance, Jamie could feel his eyes smarting. No. He couldn't let himself cry again. Not here. Not in front of the twins.

"I don't know what's going on," he said slowly. "All I know is everything about me is a lie, and the only way out is for you to forget it all and start believing what I'm telling you now."

"Tell us about the man under the tree," Megan demanded.

Jamie shrugged. "I closed my eyes and there wasn't a tree. I opened them and there was. I suppose I thought I was still half asleep. This weird man was there telling me to pick a leaf for the chance to live my lie. So I did. I mean, what would you have done? I didn't know what was going to happen. I just thought he was some nutter and I'd better get out of there."

He paused and pressed the heels of his hands into his eyes in an effort to keep back the tears.

"But as soon as I'd done it, everything was different. My whole life. Even my stupid trainers. First of all I thought maybe I'd get used to it, maybe I wouldn't have to lie anymore because suddenly I really *did* have a rich dad and I really *was* living in a big house instead of our grotty little place in Deal Street – and that was the way you all knew me."

"But we've been to your house, Jamie," interrupted Abby. "It's huge. It wouldn't even fit in Deal Street."

Despite all his efforts, that's when the tears got the better of him. Jamie leapt up.

"Oh, what's the point?" he shouted. "You're still not listening to me! We're all here because I lied to you. That's what we're living in now – my lie. It was meant to make things better but it hasn't. It's all gone wrong. Things could never have got this bad if I'd told you the truth about me in the first place. Even if you did think I was a loser, at least you wouldn't all hate me like you do now."

"We don't hate you, Jamie," said Megan gently. "But you've got to admit, it is pretty hard to swallow that this is all just some sort of bad dream."

"That's the problem," Jamie answered bitterly. "It isn't a dream. It's real. Everything that's going on is going to happen for real. My dad really is going to flatten your house, and Callum's. He really is going to build all those new houses nobody wants. He really is going to send me away to boarding school. And there's nothing I can do about it because the only way to put it all right is for you to believe me. By five o'clock tomorrow afternoon. And, let's face it, there's about as much chance of that as my mum coming back."

In the pause that followed, they were all suddenly aware of a clattering on the flat roof of the hut. The rain was picking up again.

Jamie opened the door. "I've got to get my bus or I'll be in even more trouble."

Megan stood up. "Jamie, wait."

But he didn't wait. He didn't turn around. There was nothing else he wanted to hear. And he'd got nothing left to say.

There was no-one waiting at the bus shelter over the road. The bus that picked up the after-school crowd must have gone. The next one wouldn't be for at least half an hour.

"Great," Jamie muttered as he began to trudge up the hill out of the village. Even though everyone had gone, he'd still rather use the other stop away from the school.

He had almost reached the bus pull-in when he saw a figure approaching him, hood up, head down against the rain. As they drew level, they glanced at each other briefly.

Another bad day for Jamie just got even worse.

It was Colin Renfrew.

10

Dirty work

When Philip Bryce had got back from dropping Jamie
at school that morning, he had gone straight into his
office to make a phone call. He despised people like
Colin Renfrew: petty and small-minded, and resentful
of those who'd achieved any sort of success because,
for the most part, they'd achieved nothing
themselves. Colin's big mistake was letting his anger
get the better of him. It had thrown up a weakness –
a weakness Philip Bryce was only too quick to make
use of.

Unfortunately for Colin Renfrew, Jamie's dad
knew Mark Olds, the owner of the delivery firm for
which he drove one of the blue company vans. More
than that, they were on good terms. Philip Bryce had
put quite a bit of business his way.

So it was only right that, as an employer, Mr Olds
should know the sort of man he had driving for him;
the sort of man who was a danger to himself and
others on the roads because he couldn't keep his
temper under control. Philip Bryce was doing the
delivery company a service. Road rage, he had said,

was putting it mildly.

Faced with the bedraggled form of Colin Renfrew in the narrow lane not far from where his dad had forced his van back down the hill that morning, Jamie decided the best plan was just to keep walking.

Why couldn't it have been that simple? He'd barely taken a step past him, when Colin swung round and blocked his path.

"Well, how about that?" the dripping figure murmured. "If it isn't the son of the Lord of Wellbridge himself."

Jamie tried to slip past, but Colin Renfrew was too quick and side-stepped neatly in front of him again.

"Nothing to say for yourself, Jamie? Don't you know it's very rude to ignore someone when they're talking to you?"

Jamie glanced round. There was no-one about, no-one to help him.

"All this is between you and my dad," he muttered. "It's got nothing to do with me."

"Oh, but it has," Callum's dad persisted. "Like father, like son, isn't that what they say?"

Jamie shrugged uncomfortably. He was almost within sight of the bus stop. If only the bus would come right now, he could get away. But it was too soon, and the chances were it would be late anyway.

"So tell me, Jamie, did you have a good day at

school?"

Jamie didn't respond.

"Still nothing to say?" Colin pressed on. "I know! I've got a better idea. I'll tell you about my day. Let's see, was it a good one?"

He stopped for a moment, drumming his fingers on his chin as if considering whether it had been good or bad.

"No!" he exclaimed. "I've been suspended from my job! I'm not going to get paid and I've had the van taken off me. And do you want to know why?"

Jamie's heart sank. He already knew why. He could see his dad's face as he sat in the car that morning, close to where Jamie was standing now, while Colin Renfrew hammered on his window. He could picture the jaw set rigid, the lips curled into a grim, triumphant snarl.

"Your magnificent father," Colin spat out contemptuously, "has reported me to my boss for reckless driving. He says I almost ran him off the road this morning. So now I'm on my way home to tell Callum and his mum that, not only are we losing our house, but I'm probably going to lose my job as well!"

Jamie didn't know what to say. In challenging Philip Bryce, Callum's rain-soaked dad had taken on more than he could handle. Now he'd sealed his fate. Alone in the lane with a man about to explode with barely controlled anger, Jamie began to wonder if his own wasn't sealed as well.

Just for once in its life, why couldn't the bus be early?

"Is that it then?" Colin demanded. "Stony silence? Aren't you even going to say sorry? I thought Callum was supposed to be your friend."

"He *is* my friend," Jamie murmured. "And I'm sorry about your job, but what can *I* do about it?"

"What can you do?" Callum's dad put his face close to Jamie's. Even with his hood up, Jamie could see the pulse throbbing in his temples.

"You can go and see my boss and tell him what a liar your dad is. You can tell him what really happened this morning. It was hardly reckless driving, was it?"

Jamie shook his head and tried again to walk away. But this time, Colin grabbed hold of his arm.

"You're a witness, Jamie. Come on, this can be your good deed for the day. You can help me keep my job."

"I'm sorry, I can't." As Jamie spoke, he felt Colin's fingers digging deeper.

"You *won't*, you mean," he snarled. "Just like I said, like father, like son."

That was the moment when Jamie had had enough. All right, so he seemed to have landed

himself with a particularly evil dad, but how dare
Colin Renfrew compare the two of them?

In a flash of fury he tore his arm from Colin's
grasp and yelled out, "I am nothing like Philip Bryce!"

There was a second's silence as they both took in
the words. Then, somehow, Jamie managed to shove
Callum's dad out of his way and began to run for the
bus stop.

Colin was about to pursue him when the chug of
an engine lumbering up the hill behind them caused
him to stop and turn. A bus had appeared round the
bend and was plodding slowly towards them.

Jamie had heard it too. He completed his sprint to
the pull-in running backwards and waving his arms
wildly at the driver. The bus was an unlikely escape
vehicle but to Jamie, right now it was the best thing
in the world.

It was gone. Any chance Jamie had left of making
things right with Callum had just been blown apart.
With only twenty-four hours to go, almost exactly,
until the truth counted for nothing, his dad had just
smashed the one tiny glimmer of hope he'd been
clinging on to that maybe, just maybe, he could still
win over his friends in time – all of them.

When he got home, he could hear voices behind his
dad's office door. He didn't bother to knock to say he

was home. And the last thing he was going to do was mention his encounter with Callum's dad.

He was about to shut his bedroom door when there was a loud burst of laughter. It didn't take much imagination to work out that Philip Bryce was probably taking great pleasure in sharing the news about Colin Renfrew with whichever business acquaintance he was entertaining.

Jamie let his rucksack fall to the floor and collapsed onto his bed. The first thought to strike him was that, if he did end up stuck in this grim reality – which was getting more and more likely with every passing second – he couldn't stay with his dad and he certainly couldn't let himself be sent away to boarding school. His mum was out there somewhere. She had to be. If he went looking, perhaps he could find her.

The second thought that leapt into his frantic head was just as unrealistic, but would at least mean that maybe there was still a small chance of getting Callum on his side. Colin Renfrew was a good dad, Jamie was sure of that. Maybe he'd tell Callum's mum about his suspension from work but not mention it to Callum straight away so as not to worry him even more. Losing their house was enough for him to deal with for now. Of course Jamie wasn't likely to know until the morning. He could give it one

more go. If he walked into school the next day and
things looked bad, perhaps that was the time to head
off in search of his mum.

There were voices in the corridor outside Jamie's
bedroom. He listened as they headed downstairs.
Then a car door slammed and he rolled over to look
out of his window. His dad's meeting had finished and
a bearded man was starting up the engine. As he
drove away, Jamie heard his dad call up the stairs,
"Jamie? You back yet?"

He wished he didn't have to answer, but he
answered anyway.

"Yeah."

"I'm just popping out," was the reply. "Chris is
gardening down by the quads if you need him. Be
about an hour."

Almost at the same time, Jamie's phone bleeped
telling him he had a text. He dug his hand in his
pocket and pulled out the mobile. For a moment his
eyes couldn't believe what they were seeing.

*Meet me. Central car park by bottle banks. 10 mins.
Don't tell ur dad.*

The message was from Callum.

Jamie read it over several times. He was so
stunned that Callum was actually communicating

with him, he could hardly take it in. Did he want to see Jamie because at last he was prepared to listen? Had he decided that even Jamie couldn't make up a story as bizarre as that so it must be the truth? Or was it the exact opposite? He'd heard about his dad's job and wanted to tell Jamie he'd rather die than have anything to do with him ever again.

Jamie looked at his watch. Would he even be able to get to the car park and back, *and* talk to Callum before his dad got home? Whatever happened, there was no time to stop and think. He had to leave now. He could worry about what Callum might be going to say on the way.

He tore downstairs and grabbed his bike from the rack. The ground outside was soaking but at least the rain had stopped. As he began to hurtle down the drive, he was fairly sure Chris hadn't spotted him. In seconds he'd slipped into the traffic heading for town.

If Jamie had been walking past Callum's house when Colin Renfrew got home, he would have known there was no hope of Callum not finding out about his dad's job.

Colin was fuming, even more so after his encounter with Jamie. He had shouted about the day's events so loudly to his wife that it would have been impossible for anyone passing by on the pavement not to have overheard, let alone a ten-year-old boy upstairs in his bedroom.

Mrs Renfrew sat down at the kitchen table with her head in her hands. When Colin looked up, he found Callum standing in the doorway.

"You won't really lose your job will you, Dad?" Callum's voice sounded small. Frightened.

"Yes, Callum," Colin muttered, suddenly sorry that he hadn't been able to keep his voice down. "Yes, I probably will if your mate, Jamie's, dad's got anything to do with it."

Callum shook his head. "He's not my mate."

"Yeah, well, don't you worry about it." Colin glanced back at his wife. "Plenty of other jobs out there."

They exchanged an empty smile. Callum wasn't sure whether that was for his benefit or their own. He disappeared back upstairs to try and do some work on a history project but it was a waste of time. He couldn't concentrate. When he went down to the kitchen twenty minutes later for a drink, his mum was busily scrubbing potatoes at the sink. But her eyes were red and puffy and he knew she'd been crying.

So Callum made up his mind. Everything had felt horrible since they'd found out their home was to be flattened. Now things had just got a million times worse. And it was all because of Jamie's dad.

In his bedroom, Callum emptied the contents of his moneybox into his hand and stuffed the coins into his pocket. It was probably just enough.

"I'm going round to Max's," he said briefly.

His mum looked up from the saucepan she was stirring. "Well, don't be long. Supper's nearly ready."

Callum nodded. But he didn't really know how long he was going to be. He wasn't going to Max's. He was going to walk up the hill, catch the town bus and go and see Jamie. He'd text him on the way to tell Jamie where to come and meet him. He knew he'd be in trouble for it afterwards, but if he told his mum where he was going, she'd stop him.

"Callum." He turned back at the front door and looked into his mum's worried face.

"Don't mention anything about Dad's job. This is just between us, all right? We'll sort it out, I promise."

No, Callum thought as he headed off down the road, *I'll* sort it out.

It was after five o'clock and the car park was virtually empty. Jamie couldn't see any sign of Callum. He leaned his bike against one of the two bottle banks at the far end. Then he heard something. Almost at once he was grabbed from behind and dragged backwards into the gap between the two banks. Hot, clenched fists pushed him hard up against one of the scuffed and dented metal walls.

The face shoved into Jamie's was pale and tense, the lips twisted. Callum's expression was exactly the same as his dad's when Jamie had run into him a short time before. It told Jamie everything. His worst fears were realised. This meeting had nothing to do with Callum wanting to listen to the truth.

"Do you have any idea what your dad's done?" Callum hissed. He stood so close, Jamie could almost taste the bitterness in the words.

It was pointless to pretend he didn't know.

"My dad's going to lose his job because of your dad."

Callum's fists were still rammed into Jamie's chest.

"I know," he murmured. What else could he say?

"Is that it?" stormed Callum. "That's the best you can do? We've never done anything to you! Why are you trying to ruin our lives? Why do you hate us so much?"

"I don't hate you."

"You must do! You've spoilt everything. It was all right until you came."

Callum stopped for a moment. He was out of breath. His fury seemed to have sucked the air out of his lungs. When he spoke again, his voice was barely more than a whisper.

"My mum's at home crying. Have you ever seen *your* mum crying, Jamie? Oh no, I forgot. She left, didn't she? Well, you know what? It serves you right!"

Now it was Jamie's turn to shout. Scream at him, yes, blame him for everything. After all, it really was his fault. But *don't* bring his mum into it.

With a surge of anger, he swung his arms up, knocking Callum's fists away from his chest.

"What happened with my mum's got nothing to do with you!" he yelled.

"No?" Callum snarled. He'd found his voice again. "Well my mum crying has got *everything* to do with you! And you're going to stop it. My dad's not losing his job because you're going to persuade *yours* to change his story."

Jamie shook his head. No-one persuaded his dad to do what he didn't want to do. Not *this* dad.

"Dad does what he wants. Nothing I say will make

any difference."

"Then *you* go and tell them what really happened," Callum scowled. "You were there, Dad's boss will listen to you."

"Listen to *me* over my dad?" Jamie nearly laughed. "I don't think so."

"You think it's funny, do you?" Suddenly Callum was shoving him again. "You got us into this, *you* get us out of it!"

"I've been *trying* to get you out of it. All of you. And me!"

The frustration inside Jamie exploded.

"Do you think this is what I want? To turn my best friends into deadly enemies because of things I can't do anything about? It wasn't meant to be like this. It was a lie, that's all, a good story because that was better than you knowing the truth about me."

For an instant Callum looked almost bewildered.

"What is wrong with you? My dad could lose his job and you're still going on about this truth and lies stuff. Why?"

"Because that's all this is – a lie!" Jamie shouted. "A lie that got out of control."

He felt his body sag. He'd been over it so many times. He was exhausted. He wasn't even sure he believed it himself anymore.

"Listen, Cal. I *can* sort this, but not on my own. If I

talk to my dad or your dad's boss it won't make any difference. The only way out is for me to tell *you* the truth, which is what I'm doing. And even that isn't enough on its own. For everything to come right again, you've got to believe me."

Callum was staring at him scornfully, but Jamie wasn't going to be put off. This might be the last chance he'd have to talk to him.

"I know it all sounds crazy, but I'm telling you, the future's up to *you* now. If you still think I'm a liar then…I may as well just forget the truth and go on lying because from now on, things are going to get a lot worse."

The two boys were both so wrapped up in their argument that neither of them was aware of the car that had pulled up alongside the bottle banks.

"Well, well, well."

At the sound of the voice, they both spun round. Philip Bryce stood at the opening between the banks.

"You were right, Leah," he called over his shoulder. "You did spot Jamie. Funny. There I was thinking I'd left him in his room doing his homework."

"Dad…" Jamie faltered.

But his dad wasn't going to let him speak – at least not until *he* wanted him to.

"Save it, Jamie."

He sighed and folded his arms deliberately. "So, what's this all about then? I thought I told you I didn't want you having anything to do with Callum. Yet, here you are."

"Why did you make my dad lose his job?" Callum blurted out. He knew he should probably keep quiet, but he couldn't help himself.

"I didn't," Jamie's dad shrugged. "Is that what you think? I simply pointed out to his boss that he was a danger to other people using the roads."

"But, he's a driver," Callum went on. "He delivers stuff. He won't be allowed to do it anymore."

Philip Bryce gazed at him disinterestedly. "Not really my problem."

Callum wasn't going to let it go. "But he didn't do anything."

"Ah, but he did." With that, Jamie's dad's eyes slid dangerously towards his son. "Didn't he, Jamie?"

No! Jamie's stomach tightened. That wasn't fair.

"Tell him, son. Tell him how his father nearly ran us off the road."

Jamie looked down at the ground.

"I don't know what happened," he managed to mumble. "I wasn't really looking."

He didn't see the angry glint flash into his dad's eyes but he knew it would be there.

"You'd better get off home, Callum," Philip Bryce

warned. "I'm not sure your dad would approve of you hanging around bottle banks in car parks. Unless, of course, he sent you to do his dirty work for him."

Callum glanced at Jamie whose eyes were still fixed on the ground.

That was the end of it then. He'd got nowhere.

He pushed past Jamie but the menacing figure of his father still blocked the way.

"You stay away from my son from now on, Callum, do you understand me?"

"Or what?" Callum wanted to ask. Instead he gave a very slight and sullen nod of his head. Philip Bryce stood back leaving just enough room for him to squeeze by.

As Callum crossed the car park towards the bus stop, he wondered what would happen to Jamie when he got home. For a moment he almost felt sorry for him.

At the car park entrance he glanced back. Jamie was cycling towards the far exit. Callum saw him snatch a quick look at his dad before he turned onto the main road and headed home. Philip Bryce was standing by his car watching him go. His mobile phone was pressed to his ear.

"You've got ten minutes to get home, Jamie. Be there by the time we get back."

That's all Jamie's dad had said to him as Callum had walked away.

Jamie didn't need ten minutes. He pedalled at full pelt and didn't even ease up on the downhill stretch that swept past his driveway.

Supper that evening was a silent meal. The only words spoken were by his dad to Leah as Jamie left the table and made his way upstairs to his bedroom.

"Fabels will sort him out," he heard his dad say. "They won't stand for any of his nonsense there."

"That's not till September, Phil."

"It'll come round, sweetheart."

"Yeah," Leah grimaced, "just not soon enough for me."

Jamie's dad didn't defend him, didn't tell this woman who had nothing to do with him not to talk like that about his son. He simply smiled, leaned over and gave her a sympathetic kiss.

In his room, Jamie pulled his mobile out of his pocket. He switched it off and dropped it onto the bed. He couldn't even think straight anymore. The last thing he needed was more messages.

The screen cleared momentarily. Then, for some reason, the phone burst back into life. Jamie frowned. Perhaps he hadn't pressed the button hard enough. This time he gave it a deep dig with his thumb. Once more, the screen went blank, but Jamie had hardly

tossed the mobile down before it had switched itself
back on again.

Curious, he knelt down and turned it slowly
towards him on the bed. There was a text waiting.
Odd. He hadn't heard his phone bleep since the
message from Callum. The words flipped onto the
screen.

*Don't forget, Jamie. Tomorrow 5 o'clock. See you
under the tree. And if you've managed to persuade
your friends you're telling the truth, make sure you
bring them with you. If they believe you, I need to hear
it from them. Clock's ticking.*

Jamie had been wondering whether the stranger
would contact him again before his seven-day trial
was up. He couldn't reply. The sender was unknown
so there was no number. Even if he could have texted
back, there would have been nothing to say.

For a few moments, he continued to gaze at the
message blankly. He was too tired even to feel angry.
Then, with a sense of defeat, he stood up and let the
phone drop from his fingers.

Fine. He'd go to school the next day but for the last
time, and only to keep things looking normal. If he
simply didn't show up, Mrs Steed would contact his
dad to say he hadn't appeared and find out where he

was. Jamie didn't want Philip Bryce knowing he'd disappeared until he'd had time to get far away. He could creep out tomorrow night. No-one would discover he was gone until morning.

Yes. Once he'd met the stranger at five o'clock at the old barn, he was as good as out of there.

There was a rucksack in his wardrobe. It was bigger than his school bag. Jamie pulled it out and started packing.

11

Tick tock

"What's going on, Jamie? What's happened?"

Max, Abby and Megan were waiting for him by the staff car park when he cycled in through the school gate the following morning.

"What's happened where?" Jamie answered moodily.

Max eyed him suspiciously.

"Cal says he's grounded," he said.

Jamie shrugged. "So?"

"*So*," snapped Abby, "he's hardly talking to us. He says if we want to know anything to ask you."

"I can't think why," Jamie muttered. "No-one believes a word *I* say."

"Well maybe it's about time we did."

Jamie glanced up to find Megan watching him intently.

Then he shook his head.

"That's easy to say."

"No, Jamie, I mean it," Megan insisted. "Everything's gone crazy this week. Nothing good's happened. Even last weekend something was wrong.

I mean, we all had a great time but you were acting really weird. And now something's gone bad with Cal."

Jamie said nothing and started to thread his bike lock through the front wheel.

"Oh, come on," said Max. "This is Callum we're talking about. He *never* gets grounded. What have you done?"

Jamie was losing patience. He didn't want to be in school. He didn't really want to be on the planet, and he certainly didn't want to be having this conversation. He snapped the lock together, then straightened up.

"I did what he asked me to do, all right?"

"Cal went out yesterday evening and told his mum he was going round to our house," Max persisted. "The next thing, she was getting a phone call from your dad saying he'd just seen him in town hanging around in the car park, and she ought to start keeping better tabs on him before he landed himself in real bother."

So that was the phone call Jamie had seen his dad make as he'd cycled across the car park yesterday evening. Philip Bryce had even found a way to make trouble for Callum.

He sighed heavily then said, "Cal's dad's got a problem with work so Cal asked me to meet him. He wanted me to help sort it. We didn't tell anyone what we were doing and my dad caught us."

Abby frowned. "How could *you* help?"

"Because," answered Jamie, "surprise, surprise, my dad caused the problem."

"Your dad's caused everyone's problems," muttered Megan.

"But that's just it," Jamie groaned, "that's what I keep telling you, but you won't listen. It's not him, it's *me*. This is all *my* fault."

The first bell rang for registration. The four of them barely heard it.

That's when Jamie remembered.

"Of course!" he cried, his eyes lighting up. How could he have forgotten?

"The text! Now you'll *have* to believe me."

His fingers dived into the side pocket of his rucksack and he pulled out his phone.

"What text?" Megan asked. "What are you talking about?"

"Last night, I got a text," Jamie answered excitedly. "I got a text from the man I met."

The twins exchanged a doubtful glance with Max, but Jamie didn't notice. He was already punching buttons eagerly. The text screen flashed up – and Jamie's face fell.

The last text received was Callum's telling him to

meet him in the car park. The stranger's simply wasn't there.

"No!" Jamie shook his head disbelievingly. "It's gone. How can it be gone?"

"Maybe you deleted it," Abby suggested.

"I didn't delete it!" he shouted angrily. "It should still be here! Why isn't it here? If you read it you'd know I wasn't making this up."

"What did it say?" Megan asked hesitantly.

Jamie was still desperately trying to find the message. "It said I had to meet him under the tree at five o'clock today. And you've all got to be there too."

There was a moment's silence. Max and the twins watched Jamie's thumb frantically scrolling through the menus.

"I suppose it wouldn't really prove anything," said Megan slowly. "I mean you could have sent yourself a text."

Almost as soon as she'd said it, she wished she hadn't.

Jamie stopped dead and looked at her. The colour seemed to be draining from his eyes.

"Of course," he said coldly. "Of course, that's what I did. I sent myself a text. Then, just so I'd look even more stupid, I told you about it but deleted it before you'd had a chance to read it!"

"Jamie," Max began, "she didn't mean..."

"Save it, Max," Jamie interrupted. "I know exactly what she meant."

He snatched up his rucksack, shoved the phone back in the pocket, then pushed past them up the path towards the cloakroom entrance.

But in those last few moments, they'd all seen something in his face. Something they couldn't ignore.

They'd seen the truth.

"Jamie!" Max yelled. Jamie didn't stop.

"If we come with you at five o'clock," he carried on, "we'll see him too, won't we? We'll see this man you keep going on about."

This was enough to make Jamie hesitate. He half turned his head.

"Yeah," he replied flatly. "No...I don't know, I suppose so."

He felt nothing. It was too good to be true. They'd never come.

The second bell rang out across the playground.

Max caught him up and examined his face. He'd never seen Jamie look so tired.

"You really believe in this lying tree stuff, don't you?" he said.

Jamie nodded bitterly. "Why would I make it up?"

"According to you," reminded Max, "you've made up your whole life."

Max glanced back at the twins. As soon as he looked at them he knew they were all thinking the same thing.

"Like you said ages ago," he said finally, "if we believe you we've got nothing to lose. We'll come with you after school."

Jamie stared at him blankly. It took a moment for the words to sink in. After all this, was it going to be all right? Finally he managed a half-hearted yet grateful smile.

But it quickly faded on his lips.

"What about Cal?" he asked grimly. "It's got to be him as well. Otherwise whatever *you* believe, it's a waste of time."

"I'll talk to him," Max replied. There was real determination in his voice. "I'll make him understand."

Megan shook her head doubtfully. "He'll only believe it if he sees this man for himself, and he's grounded. Even if he agreed to come with us, he wouldn't be able to. Not unless you can persuade his parents as well."

"We'll think of something," Max said. "We've got to."

None of them had noticed Mrs Steed watching them from the top of the playground.

"Why are you still out here? The second bell went

ages ago."

Her voice boomed out in the grating way it always did when she was annoyed, yet today there was something strangely comforting about it. In Mrs Steed's world at least, everything was normal.

The morning dragged on endlessly. There was no sign of Callum at break. Max looked everywhere. It wasn't until lunchtime that he finally managed to corner him in the cloakroom.

He waited until they were on their own, then stood right behind him and said, "We've got to talk."

Callum was fishing his lunch box out of his bag.

"I told you," he answered sullenly. "Talk to Jamie. He's the one with all the answers."

"We *have* talked to Jamie," Max announced. "And we've made a decision."

Callum pulled out a plastic box, snapped off the lid and took out a biscuit. He didn't show the slightest interest, but Max ignored him and carried on.

"We're going to believe him, Cal. We're going to believe what Jamie's been saying."

Very deliberately, Callum put the lid back on the box and stuffed it into his bag again.

"Do you know how lame that sounds?" he smirked. "You don't just 'decide' to believe someone, Max. You either believe him or you don't. And I don't."

Max wasn't going to be put off. "You didn't see him this morning. He said he'd had a text from this man he keeps talking about. But when he went to show us, it wasn't there."

"That's because there wasn't any text."

"No, Cal," Max insisted, "he really thought there was. I've never seen him like that. He wasn't pretending."

Callum didn't reply so Max went on, "Jamie wants to make things right, I know he does. But he can't do it without us. All of us. That means you too."

"Give me one good reason why I should do anything for him."

"You won't be doing it for him," Max said quietly. "You'll be doing it for yourself. And for Abby and Megan. You want to keep your house, don't you? It's got to be worth a try."

Callum looked at him incredulously.

"Jamie's mental, Max! How can you possibly believe that he picked some lie off a tree?"

Max hesitated. Callum was right. But it wasn't just Jamie. The whole thing was mental. Maybe that was exactly why they had to believe in it.

"I don't know," he said at last. "But Jamie believes it, and you know what? Right now that's enough for me."

The door swung open. Miss Kendal, their form

teacher, stood in front of them.

"Come on, you boys, you know you're not supposed to hang around in here," she said. "Go outside and get some fresh air."

They wandered out into the playground. There was the usual haphazard tearing around, skipping ropes twirling, footballs punching through the air. But for once, Max wasn't interested in joining in.

He knew he was losing the argument, but he had to give it one last try.

"Jamie met you in the car park yesterday, Cal. He didn't have to, but he did."

"Yeah," Callum muttered, "and look where that got me – grounded."

"But why would he bother if he was just messing you about? I know he's acting freaky but, the least we can do is give him a chance."

A football smacked into the wall next to them and bounced off onto Callum's shins. There was a shout of "Callum, over here!" Callum gave it a hard kick, sending it spinning back to the group of boys playing on the field.

Max watched his face anxiously.

"You know what, you're absolutely right," Callum said at last. "Jamie is definitely freaky."

With that, he wandered away.

"Well?" demanded Megan, running up to Max with

Abby close behind. Max shook his head dejectedly.

"Callum's such an idiot," said Abby crossly.

"Maybe we're the ones who are the idiots," grumbled Max and headed inside.

12

Head on

It was P.E. The final session of the day. The final session of the *final day*, Jamie thought. He looked at the clock. Quarter past two. Less than three hours until his bizarre deadline. Until he was trapped in this nightmare forever. Max followed him into the changing room but Jamie didn't bother to ask how it was going with Callum. He could see from his face that he'd got nowhere.

As he got changed, he felt empty. Callum was ignoring him in the opposite corner. He didn't even glance Jamie's way.

When the class sat on the floor in the hall a few minutes later, with Miss Kendal explaining that today they were going to explore balance, neither he nor Jamie, nor Max and the twins took in a word.

Until, that is, the names Jamie and Callum were called out.

Suddenly, Miss Kendal had their full attention.

"Come on then," she chivvied. "It's about time you two did some work today. Let's see if you can show us some examples of balance."

Jamie gave Callum a cautious glance, but Callum refused to look at him. Neither of them moved.

"I'm sorry, I can't, Miss," Callum said.

"Don't be silly, of course you can, come on."

That was all Miss Kendal said. There was no getting out of it. Did she know what was going on? Was this her clumsy attempt at putting things right between them?

If only it was that simple, Jamie thought.

The two boys stood up awkwardly and walked to the front.

"Any kind of balance," Miss Kendal continued. "It could be a balance where you're relying on each other to hold each other up, or, say, a balancing shape, something symmetrical. Use your imagination."

Considering it was his imagination that had got him into this mess, Jamie wasn't inclined to use it ever again. But he had to do something. Without even thinking about balance, he stretched out his arms to the sides. One hand reached hesitantly towards Callum. Under the scrutiny of Miss Kendal and the rest of the class, at least Callum couldn't ignore him. Reluctantly and without looking him in the eye, Callum grasped hold of Jamie's hand and stretched his other arm sideways to mirror his move.

"That's it." Miss Kendal sounded pleasantly surprised. "Now, if you each lean out and pull away from each other, you'll create a balance. You'll be holding each other up."

Holding each other up? Jamie sighed inwardly. That sounded like a bad idea. With anyone else, maybe. But not Callum. Not today.

Miss Kendal was waiting. Very slowly, Jamie began to lean away. Callum felt his body weight pulling on his arm. For a moment he started to lean out too and Jamie's grip tightened on his hand.

Then Callum let go. The timing was perfect. Without warning, he suddenly loosened his fingers. Jamie was leaning too far out to save himself, and he fell sideways with a painful thud, landing on his wrist awkwardly. Laughter rippled across the hall.

"Callum!" shouted Miss Kendal. "The idea is to hold on to each other."

"Sorry, Miss," he said. "My hand slipped."

Jamie got up, rubbing his wrist.

"You've got to be more careful," she continued crossly. "Come on then, let's try another one."

Another one? How many more chances was she going to give Callum to flatten him?

"I've hurt my wrist," Jamie said quietly.

"Oh, come on," dismissed Miss Kendal. "We're going to make up a sequence in a moment."

She stood watching him expectantly.

And she wasn't the only one. When Jamie looked

round, his eyes met Callum's. The glimmer of triumph was unmistakeable. Callum knew he was about to get the upper hand.

"What about facing each other and leaning out backwards?" suggested Miss Kendal briskly.

What about getting off my case? Jamie thought.

The boys moved to stand opposite each other about a metre apart.

"No, no, no!" Miss Kendal grumbled, grasping Jamie's shoulders and pushing him closer to Callum. "Right, now hold on to each other's hands and see how far you can lean out."

It was a bit like being ordered to walk the plank. As Jamie began to lean cautiously backwards, he fixed his eyes on Callum's face, trying to anticipate the exact moment when his angry partner might let him go, to save himself another smack on the floor. Max was watching him too. Jamie wasn't the only one who knew this wasn't a good idea.

"All right," said Miss Kendal. "Now, Jamie, try letting go of Callum's left hand with your right hand, then both of you twist the top half of your bodies round to face outwards."

How do teachers come up with these things? More to the point, *why* do teachers come up with these things?

Reluctantly, still leaning back, Jamie braced himself

ready for the twist out. Then he dropped Callum's left hand. He felt his stomach muscles tense as he made the move, but only for an instant. In that split second, Callum had opened the fingers of his supporting hand and pulled them away. Jamie crashed down, this time onto his elbow. There was a second eruption of laughter around the hall.

"That's enough!" Miss Kendal shouted.

Callum was smirking.

"Whoops!" he sneered. "I must have let go with the wrong hand."

Miss Kendal's patience had just snapped.

"Concentrate on what you're doing and stop messing around, both of you," she huffed, "or you can both sit out for the rest of the lesson."

If he had to keep working with Callum, sitting out sounded like Jamie's only chance of escaping a broken neck.

But Miss Kendal seemed to have finished with the demonstrations.

"I'm sure you all get the idea," she said, addressing the rest of the class, "so find a partner and work on some balances. When you've found a few different ones, you can start putting them together in a sequence."

Jamie and Callum got up to join the others, but Miss Kendal stopped them. They'd annoyed her and she wasn't in the mood to let it go.

"Where do you think you're going? You two can carry on working together. And do try and come up with something that doesn't involve Jamie Bryce being dropped on the floor. The idea is to rely on each other for support, all right?"

No, it wasn't all right. How do you rely on someone who obviously hates your guts? Jamie thought for a moment then knelt down on the floor. He looked up at Callum hoping he'd follow, but he just stood there.

"We've got to do this," Jamie muttered, aware of Miss Kendal's watchful eyes, "so we may as well get on with it." There was no response.

He tried again. "We could try one of those leaning out things down here."

"Why?" Callum scowled. "So you don't have so far to fall when I drop you?"

Jamie was running out of everything. Energy. Patience. Interest. He was even beginning to wonder why he was bothering to try and help Callum at all.

"Look, all I want to do is put things right," he sighed wearily. "Why are you making it so hard?"

"I'm just letting you know what it feels like to be *let down*." Callum gritted his teeth and spat the words out spitefully.

This was too much. Before he could stop himself, Jamie had sprung to his feet. The next minute, Callum lay sprawled on the floor, knocked flying as Jamie ran into him and shoved him across the hall with all the strength he had left.

"I may have let you down," he screamed, "but at least I've got the guts to admit it!"

All movement in the hall froze. The only sound was Jamie's breathing as an overload of frustration pumped the air in and out of his lungs.

"Jamie! Callum! Come here now!" Miss Kendal's voice sliced through the stillness but the two boys didn't seem to hear.

Callum scrambled to his feet. His face was red. He was fuming.

"You haven't got the guts to do anything!" he yelled. "You can't even stand up to your own dad!"

"I don't need to stand up to him!" Jamie blurted out. "I can sort all this out another way but *you* won't let me. And anyway, he's *not* my dad!"

There was a deathly silence. Nobody moved.

"I know what this is about." Miss Kendal stood over them. Her voice was deliberately quiet.

"Well, I won't have it in my class, do you understand? Now, both of you stand over there by the door and if I hear another word you'll go straight to Mrs Steed. And she may decide to contact your parents."

They did as they were told. The threat of Mrs Steed didn't bother Jamie too much, but he didn't want Philip

Bryce hearing about this. Nothing was going to spoil his escape plans.

The excitement over, the other children returned to stretching and bending, twisting their bodies into curious shapes like an odd array of tentacled plants on the seabed, waving and writhing with the rhythm of the tide.

Jamie had to get out – out of the hall, out of school, far away from everyone.

Callum was never going to believe a word he said. It was pointless to stick around even till five o'clock. Jamie had lost and the stranger had won. As soon as school was over, he'd cycle home, grab his money and the bag he'd packed last night. He didn't know where he was going, but it didn't matter. All he wanted was to get away. Far away.

It had been a difficult afternoon at the end of a long week for Miss Kendal. She stood militantly outside the changing rooms, arms folded. The balancing lesson hadn't gone well. If she heard one word out of anyone, she'd threatened, the entire class would stay in every lunchtime next week.

The silence was resounding.

Jamie didn't want to talk anyway. As he got changed, he was trying to work out his next move. He was already wishing he'd decided not to go into school that morning. If he'd set off first thing, he'd still have been able to get a bit of a head start before Mrs Steed telephoned his dad and a search began. Now he couldn't stand the thought of having to hang around until the middle of the night. He had to go now.

But how was he going to get his bag out of the house and then make a break for it on his bike without his dad noticing? Even through the closed door of his office, Philip Bryce seemed to sense everything that went on. Jamie had to go home, though. He'd brought nothing with him. If nothing else, he needed his money.

In the corner of the changing room, Callum kept trying to catch Jamie's eye. It was no good. Jamie wasn't even thinking about him. But if he'd looked at Callum as they'd stood together by the hall door not long before, while the rest of the class worked on balancing, he would have been surprised at the expression on his face. Callum didn't know why he was feeling the way he did. He couldn't work it out. None of what Jamie said made any sense. How could anyone believe in the ridiculous story he kept telling?

And yet, in that instant when Jamie had screamed out that Philip Bryce wasn't his dad, Callum had seen what Max and the twins already knew. Bizarre as it was, there was total belief in his face and voice. Jamie was telling the truth.

Back in the classroom, the bell finally went. Max was about to go over to Jamie when Callum hissed at him and beckoned him over.

"Don't ask me to explain it because I can't," Callum whispered. "But…I think maybe you're right. I think Jamie is telling the truth."

Max gaped at him. "Are you serious? After what just happened in the hall?"

Callum nodded. He felt stupid. "It's *because* of what just happened in the hall."

The corners of Max's mouth twitched with the beginnings of a smile.

"Well it's Jamie you should be telling," he said.

He turned towards Jamie's table, but there was no sign of him. Quickly he scanned the classroom. He wasn't there.

Max went to pick up his bag.

"Come on, we'll catch him in the cloakroom."

But although there were plenty of other jostling children in there, Jamie was nowhere to be seen. And his peg was empty.

"He can't have gone," Max frowned. "We're all supposed to be heading up to the old barn."

"What for?" Callum asked.

"That's where he's meeting that man he's always talking about. We've all got to be there. At five o'clock."

"Well I can't go anywhere. I'm grounded, remember?"

That was another problem they'd have to sort out,

but for now all Max wanted to do was find Jamie.

He pushed open the door to the playground and was almost knocked flying. Abby and Megan ran right into him.

"Where's Jamie going?" Megan panted anxiously.

Max looked puzzled.

"What do you mean?"

"We just saw him pushing his bike down to the gate."

"*What?*" he cried. "No, he's supposed to be waiting for us!"

Max threw down his bag and hurtled across the playground. He just had time to catch a glimpse of Jamie in the distance, head down, pedalling away towards town before he disappeared round the corner.

"Jamie!" He yelled so loudly that children and waiting parents turned to look. If Jamie heard, he took no notice.

The others caught up with Max.

"Where's he gone?" asked Abby breathlessly.

"I don't know. He must be heading home."

"Home?" cried Megan. "He can't be."

"Oh no, there's my dad," Callum moaned. "I've got to go."

"Well it doesn't really matter, does it?" Abby glared at him. "You don't believe us anyway!"

"Yes, I do!" he snapped. "That's what I've been

telling Max. But I can't come with you to the barn."

Suddenly Max turned on him.

"This is all *your* fault," he shouted. "Jamie would have waited for us if it hadn't been for you. Why couldn't you just have gone along with him?"

"Don't you think we've already wasted enough time arguing?" Abby interrupted. "It doesn't matter whose fault it is! We've just got to get him back here."

"How?" Max snarled. "What do you want me to do, run after him?"

"Callum! Here now!"

They all turned together. Callum's dad was glaring at them.

Abby lowered her voice.

"Text him or something, Max. Just get him back."

Colin Renfrew was on the point of coming in through the gate.

"My phone's in my bag," Max muttered sulkily and headed up the path to where he'd dropped it.

"I've got to go," Callum murmured.

"When you get home, wait for my text," Megan hissed after him.

"What?" He turned briefly.

"Wait for my text," she repeated, keeping one eye on the looming figure of Colin Renfrew. "You've got to come with us up to the old barn, haven't you? Well, we've had an idea. We think we can get you out."

13

Believe it or not

At the end of that afternoon, Jamie had been almost the first out of school. He'd pushed through the cloakroom, grabbed his jacket from his peg and was unlocking his bike within moments of the bell ringing. He didn't want to speak to anyone. He'd made up his mind he was leaving and he wasn't going to say goodbye. Not even to Max.

He'd seen the twins out of the corner of his eye as he pushed his bike down to the gate, and he knew Max had shouted to him as he pedalled away up the road. But nothing was going to stop him. He'd hung around long enough.

Halfway up the hill, his mobile buzzed agitatedly in his pocket. It was probably Max. There was no point in answering. Callum was never going to believe the truth and time had run out. Jamie's lies had destroyed everything.

He turned into the drive and cycled down towards the house. He saw at once that the Lexus wasn't parked in its usual place. At least that was one thing in Jamie's favour. His dad must be out. Maybe his escape would be easier than he thought.

In the distance, he could see Chris mowing the grass. As Jamie got off his bike and started to wheel it down the side of the house, the gardener raised his head and gave him a wave. Jamie barely lifted a hand in response. He didn't know where his dad had gone or how soon before he'd be back, but he guessed he probably wouldn't have long.

Leaning the bike against the wall by the back door, he ran in and up the stairs. His phone vibrated again but he ignored it. He grabbed the bag he'd packed the night before and slung it over his shoulder. As he gave a final glance round the room to check there was nothing he'd missed, his attention was caught briefly by something on his desk. He took a step towards it.

The leaf he had picked lay exactly where he'd dropped it that last Friday evening. It felt like a lifetime ago. Strangely, he'd almost forgotten it was there. Stranger still, it hadn't changed. Despite having no water, it had lost none of its firmness and shine. There was no sign of it even beginning to dry out.

Jamie couldn't stand the sight of it. With a swipe of his hand, he brushed it off the desk and into the wastepaper bin.

Seconds later, he was hurtling back down the

stairs. In the kitchen he hesitated. He was going to need food but he couldn't carry much. There was a packet of biscuits in the cupboard and a clump of bananas sat in the fruit bowl on the side. He grabbed them and stuffed them into his bag.

It was only as he was about to hurry back to his bike that it actually struck him.

What did he think he was doing? He was going to try to find his mum but he had absolutely no idea where to start looking. The likelihood was she didn't want him any more. Why else wouldn't she have been in touch? But even if she did, she could be anywhere. Supposing she'd left the country. No, he couldn't just run off with nothing to go on.

Jamie's mind was racing. There had to be something somewhere in this house. Some clue, a tiny snippet of information he could use as a starting point.

He tore back upstairs and into his dad's office. The filing cabinets were still locked. He pulled open the desk drawers and flicked through the contents again. Was there really any point? This was all his dad's work stuff. It would help if he knew what he was looking *for*.

When the phone on the desk started to ring, Jamie almost jumped out of his skin.

But he saw it immediately.

Underneath the
telephone was a book.
Several pieces of paper
stuck out from in amongst
the pages. The answer
phone clicked on but the
caller didn't bother to leave a
message. Careful not to disturb the receiver, Jamie
slid the book out.

It was an address book, worn and obviously well-
used, with the tabs marking the alphabetical sections
quite dog-eared. The spine was broken and as Jamie
flipped the cover back, the pages fell open at the
letter C. The spaces were filled with addresses and
phone numbers in his dad's precisely formed
handwriting. Jamie scanned down the list but the
names meant nothing.

Until the last entry. When his dad had inserted it,
there had only just been enough room. One address
had been crossed through and another squeezed in at
the bottom of the page. This second address was in
Scotland. Both were under the name Claire. No
surname, just Claire.

Jamie hadn't noticed that he'd stopped breathing.
He stood quite still staring more through the page
than at it.

His mother's name was Claire.

He tried to think logically. This Claire could be nothing to him. She could be no-one. Or...

The writing began to swim in front of his eyes. He felt dizzy. He sucked a great gasp of air into his lungs as he swayed forward, grabbing on to the oak desk to support himself.

Somewhere behind him, he was only vaguely aware of the crunch of wheels on gravel. But it was enough to shake the life back into him. Grasping the book tightly, he raced into his bedroom and peered cautiously through the window.

Philip Bryce was backing the silver Lexus into its parking space. Jamie had to get out of there. Now!

He shot back down to the kitchen, slid the address book into his bag and flew out of the back door. If he went round to the front of the house, either his dad or Chris, still cutting grass, would spot him instantly, so he pushed his bike the other way.

At the end of the path that curved away from the wooden building housing the bike rack, there were four stone steps down. Here a stretch of grass ran along by the hedge and a small gate opened onto a public footpath. Once on the path, it was only a short ride to the main road.

Jamie would have to move fast. Chris would tell his dad he'd just seen him arrive home, but in no time his dad would discover he wasn't there. Disappearing

without a word wouldn't go down well. His dad had
made it clear, especially after yesterday and the car
park incident with Callum, that he expected to be
kept informed of his every move – not because he was
concerned about him, Jamie was certain, but so that
he could keep control. And Philip Bryce wasn't the
sort of father to sit at home waiting for his son to get
back. He'd be sure to go after him.

Worse, in his hurry to get out, Jamie had forgotten
to shut the door of the office. His dad would guess
he'd been in there. He'd be livid. It would probably
take him only a few seconds to see that the address
book was missing. And if the Claire listed under C
was Jamie's mum, his dad might even work out that
he'd decided to go looking for her.

As Jamie opened the gate onto the footpath, his
phone went off again.

"Max, why don't you just give up!" he muttered
impatiently, and yanked the mobile out of his pocket
to switch it off.

But he stopped short. The call wasn't from Max at
all.

It was from Callum.

Why would Callum be phoning him? What could
he possibly have to say that hadn't been said already?
Callum hated him. In any case, with his dad about to
discover that Jamie had been poking around in his

office again, he didn't have time to talk now. His thumb hovered briefly over the off button.

But something changed his mind. If nothing else he could tell Callum one last time he was sorry.

"Yeah?" Jamie was careful to keep his voice low as he pushed open the gate and wheeled his bike on to the footpath.

"Where are you?" demanded Callum. "Have you spoken to Max?"

"What's the point?"

"What?" Callum was straining to hear.

"I said, what's the point?" Jamie repeated softly. "You all think I'm a loser."

"Can you speak up a bit? I can hardly hear you."

"I can't talk any louder," Jamie hissed in response, "and I can't talk for long."

"Good!" snapped Callum, "because I don't want you to talk at all!"

Great, Jamie thought. He'd answered his phone and all he was going to get was another tongue lashing.

"No, that's the whole problem, isn't it, Callum?" he grunted. "You've already made up your mind about me."

"Yes I have," Callum snarled back. "That's what I'm trying to tell you, idiot! I believe you. I believe what you've been saying. Don't ask me why, but I do."

Jamie, who'd been about to climb on his bike and head along the path for the main road, stopped dead. For an instant he stood silent, too stunned to speak.

"Jamie. Jamie, are you listening to me?" Callum growled urgently.

"Yeah," Jamie managed.

"Right. Megan says she and Abby have got some way of getting me out of the house. So get yourself up to the old barn and we'll meet you there. And Jamie," he added, "get a move on. If this five o'clock deadline's for real we've got less than an hour. Don't let us down."

Then he was gone.

Jamie stood gazing at the phone blankly. If he'd been confused before, now he was totally baffled. Was this Callum's idea of a joke? It couldn't be real, could it? What on earth would have made him change his mind?

Jamie knew he should have been ecstatic. He *would* have been had it been an hour earlier.

But it wasn't. The strange man, the Lying Tree, saving his friends – at the last minute, all of it had been unexpectedly taken over by something else. In the rucksack slung loosely on his back was perhaps another way out for Jamie. A clue that might lead him to the one person he thought he'd never see again – in the old life or the new one: his mum. The entry in the address book might take him to his mum.

He looked at his watch. Ten minutes past four. He still just about had time to get to the barn as long as his dad didn't catch up with him.

Meeting the stranger there with his four friends and returning the lie would mean escaping back to his old life, putting everything right – which was what he wanted...wasn't it? That's what he'd spent the last few days fighting for.

But that was before he'd discovered the address book. In his old life, his other dad never talked about his mum. He never even mentioned her. As far as Jamie knew, he hadn't a clue where she was. This might be his only chance of ever finding her again. How could he throw that away? On the other hand, how could he throw away his friends? Had he really worked so hard at winning back their trust simply to let them down again?

Jamie's phone vibrated for what seemed like the hundredth time since he'd cycled away from school. What now? He frowned down at the screen.

But this was a call he definitely wasn't going to take. It was Philip Bryce.

Philip Bryce would have discovered by now that Jamie wasn't there. He'd be bound to have noticed his open office door and, more than likely, the missing address book. He might even have flung open the wardrobe in Jamie's bedroom and found some of his clothes missing. Jamie could picture his jaw set rigid, his eyes glinting with anger.

That's when he made up his mind.

It wasn't so much the horrible thought that if he stayed here in his twisted little lie, he'd always have the shadow of this Philip Bryce lurking somewhere behind him. It was the realisation that, if he didn't go home, he'd never see his real dad ever again. And suddenly, it was his real dad he wanted to be with more than anyone else in the world.

Not only that, but this wasn't just about him. It was about saving his friends. About telling the truth and putting things right. He'd got them all into this. Whatever it took, it was up to him to get them all out.

He jabbed the phone off with his thumb, thrust it in his pocket and got on his bike. Ahead of him lay the main road. At the junction, he slipped into the steady stream of traffic grinding along towards the town.

Jamie was glad it was busy. He could sneak in and out of the queues that began to build quickly at this time of day, but if his dad decided to drive towards Wellbridge in search of him, he should get conveniently stuck.

"Are Megan and Abby home?"

When the twins' mum had opened the front door a short time earlier, she'd found Max on the doorstep looking hot and flustered.

"Yes, Max," she answered. "Not sure what they're up to. They disappeared upstairs the moment they got in."

She hesitated and looked at him more closely.

"Are you all right?"

"Yeah," said Max trying to sound casual, "just, you know, homework stuff."

The twins' mum raised her eyebrows.

"On a Friday afternoon?" she smiled. "Well *you're* keen. You'd better go on up."

At the top of the stairs, Max knocked on the bedroom door and Megan whipped it open. Before he could say a word, she'd grabbed his arm and pulled him inside. Abby was at the computer. She glanced round briefly but didn't stop typing.

"Where's Jamie?" Megan demanded.

Max shook his head miserably.

"I keep texting and I've left messages, but he won't answer. I don't even know if his phone's on."

"Then you're just going to have to get over there!" Megan ordered crossly.

"There isn't time," Max moaned. We've only got till five o'clock, remember. It's after four now."

"Finished," announced Abby triumphantly and the

printer on the table beside her began to churn out a document.

"Finished what?" Max wanted to know.

"Callum's escape plan. We're going to get him out," said Megan excitedly.

"How?"

Before either of the twins had time to answer, the mobile on Megan's bed burst into life. She snatched it up. There was a text from Callum.

J on his way. If ur getting me out of here it better be now.

14

Backfire

An alleyway ran along the end of Wellbridge Primary School field, separating it from the back gardens of the houses in School Road. It would be easy for Callum to sneak through the back door in the kitchen and out of the gate into the alley, as long as his parents were distracted by something else.

At ten minutes past four, there was a knock on Callum's front door. His dad answered it. When he saw Abby and Megan on the doorstep, he looked faintly irritated.

"Come on, girls, I'm sure you know Callum's grounded," he began, but Abby interrupted him.

"It's not Callum we want to see," she announced enthusiastically, beaming up into Colin Renfrew's frowning face. "It's you, and Mrs Renfrew if she's here. It's for homework. We have to go through a questionnaire with parents."

As if to back up what her sister had just said, Megan eagerly held up a clipboard and tapped the piece of A4 paper attached to it which she'd just printed off in their bedroom.

"It'll only take a few minutes," she bubbled. "It's about the new school."

The twins saw Colin's teeth clamp together. That was the one flaw in their plan. The school was such a hot subject in the village at the moment that, when they'd had the idea less than an hour before, they'd felt sure Callum's dad would easily believe that Mrs Steed was happily involving the children in the project. They just hoped he wouldn't be so angry about Philip Bryce's whole scheme that he'd refuse to answer the questions. If he shut the door in their faces, they'd never get Callum out.

"Hello, girls, what are you after?" Mrs Renfrew appeared from the kitchen.

"They want to ask us some questions about the new school," Colin informed her grimly.

"It's just homework," Megan explained. "We've got to collect information from all round the village about what people want from the new school - what sort of facilities they think it ought to have, that kind of thing."

She paused and looked from one to the other.

"We promise it won't take long."

Mrs Renfrew glanced at her husband then sighed, "Go on then."

"Great, thanks!" Abby beamed. It was working.

"Number one," said Megan, her pencil poised to tick

the relevant box. "Do you think the new school should have a swimming pool?"

"I thought that was already decided," Colin grumbled.

"It is really, but do *you* think it should have one?" Megan pressed on. "You can answer yes, no or don't know."

"All right then, no, I don't think it should have a pool. That way maybe I could keep my house."

"Colin!" Mrs Renfrew was obviously embarrassed, but Megan pretended not to notice.

"It's all right, Mrs Renfrew," she said, "We'll just tick 'no'. You're entitled to your opinion."

She duly ticked the 'no' box and rattled on again.

"Number two. Do you think the new school should have an indoor play area for bad weather?"

Callum didn't hear his parents' response to the second question. The moment he was as certain as he could be that their attention was fully on the twins and the questionnaire they had hurriedly put together after school, he sneaked silently from the lounge into the kitchen, and out through the back door.

Max was waiting for him in the alleyway. They looked at each other and grinned. Getting out couldn't have been easier.

When Philip Bryce had arrived home that afternoon, Chris had signalled to him that Jamie had just got back. Philip Bryce had marched upstairs to find him. The first thing he'd noticed was the open door to his office. The second was the missing address book. Just as Jamie had predicted.

Jamie would never know exactly what went through his dad's mind, but, finding his son nowhere in the house and the Stumpjumper gone from the rack, he'd immediately jumped into the Lexus and headed off for Wellbridge in search of him. He was sure that's where he would be. If nothing else he could bang on the Renfrews' front door and demand to know where he'd gone. After yesterday's incident in the car park, he was absolutely certain that, if anyone knew, the useless Renfrews would.

If Callum had been able to escape from his house a few moments earlier, he and Max would have been just in time to see Jamie pedalling furiously past the school. Then Jamie would have been able to warn them to get off the road and hide because his dad was right behind him. The silver Lexus had caught up with him at almost the last set of traffic lights before the Wellbridge turning. The only reason Jamie had got away was because the driver of the car in front of his dad was a learner who stalled the engine just as the lights turned to green.

But timing wasn't on their side. Jamie was just out of sight when Max and Callum emerged from the alley. The hastily hatched plan was for them to wait for Abby and Megan up the track at the stile on the way to the old barn. The twins knew they'd have to run all the way once they'd finished going through the questionnaire – as soon as they'd closed their front door, it wouldn't take Callum's parents long to realise that they'd been tricked and he'd gone.

"So far so good," Max said to Callum briefly, but there was no time to hang about. They needed to get out of sight of Callum's house.

What happened next took them

totally by surprise.

A large silver car sped along past the end of School Road. It swerved out slightly, then, without warning, mounted the pavement in front of them, effectively blocking their path. The boys were tearing along and barely had time to stop. Max had to reach out his hands to buffer the rest of his body. They landed with a stinging smack flat against the boot.

Then the car door swung open aggressively and Philip Bryce stepped towards them.

"Well, well, well," he said, "you are in a hurry. Funny, that. My Jamie's in a right old hurry too. Where are you all off to?"

Callum shook his head.

"Nowhere," he faltered. "We were just…going to the park. We haven't seen Jamie."

"Is that right?" Philip Bryce replied flatly, examining the tense, upturned face. Then, leaning towards him he said, "You really are as pathetic as your father. Where is he, by the way? I'm surprised he's let you go roaming off after I caught you in the car park yesterday."

Callum didn't answer.

"We're only going to the park," Max gulped.

Philip Bryce's eyes slid towards him dangerously.

"Oh. Little Max has got something to say now, has he?"

He took a step closer.

"So, tell me. Where's Jamie?"

The boys exchanged a nervous glance.

"What are you asking *us* for?" Callum muttered, avoiding Jamie's dad's eyes. "We haven't had much to do with him lately."

"Of course you haven't," Philip Bryce sneered. "That's why you were sneaking around with him yesterday."

Max and Callum were beginning to panic. Not only were the seconds ticking away to the five o'clock deadline but, any minute now, Callum's parents would have finished the questionnaire. Instead of having made a clean getaway, Abby and Megan would find the boys only a few metres from the end of School Road. Callum's escape would be discovered and all four of them would be trapped on the pavement, pinned down not just by one, but by three angry parents.

Suddenly the air jangled as a mobile went off. Philip Bryce's eyes travelled to the pocket of Max's jacket.

"Aren't you going to get that?" he murmured.

Max shook his head.

"I think you should," insisted Philip Bryce. "It might be Jamie. When I know where he is, we can all be put out of our misery."

Max didn't move. Philip Bryce's eyes darkened.
"Answer it, Max."

All at once, he was interrupted by the sound of
running feet. Megan and Abby had appeared at the
end of School Road and begun to race along the
pavement.

It was Max and Callum they saw first. Puzzled,
they slowed down.

At the sight of Philip Bryce they stopped dead.

He stood right in their path.

"Come on, then," he said, folding his arms, "I want
to know what's going on and I want to know now."

The four of them looked at each other frantically.

Then an angry shout split the air.

"Callum!"

If things were bad already, they were about to get
a thousand times worse. When the children saw the
expression on Colin Renfrew's face as he appeared
round the corner, they weren't sure whose dad they
ought to be more scared of.

Abby and Megan only hesitated for a second.

Then they ran. As she leapt off the pavement to
get round the Lexus, Abby reached out her hand to
snatch Max and drag him with her, but when the
boys went to move, Philip Bryce was ready. He
grabbed hold of Max then effortlessly twisted round
and seized Callum's arm with his other hand,

yanking him backwards.

That was a mistake.

"Bryce!" bellowed Callum's dad. "Get your hands off my son!"

Jamie's dad looked up furiously.

"Do you want him to run off?" he flared without loosing his grip on either boy. "These kids are up to something and I want to know what it is."

"I'm warning you, Bryce, you take your hands off them."

The two men glared at each other for a moment. But out in the street, in full view of anyone who might be passing by, there wasn't a lot Philip Bryce could do. Grudgingly he released his hold. The boys backed away from him, Callum rubbing his upper arm where the vicious fingers had dug painfully in.

With his eyes still fixed on Philip Bryce, Colin Renfrew ordered, "I don't know what this is all about, Callum, but you get home. Now. Mr Bryce and I have things to discuss."

Callum looked desperately round at his friends. They could probably still just about make it to the old barn in time, but without him, there was no point. If ever he needed his dad to believe in him, it was now.

"Dad."

"Go home, Callum." The gritted teeth told Callum his dad was out of patience.

"Dad, I'm sorry but…I can't."

His dad's eyes flicked towards him.

Philip Bryce sniggered.

"Colin Renfrew," he smirked, "the ex-delivery boy who can't even control his own son."

Callum saw the fury flash across his dad's face. Without stopping to think, he stepped between him and Philip Bryce.

"Don't listen to him, Dad," he blurted out, "you're not an ex anything. After this I promise I'll do everything you say. You can ground me for the rest of my life. But, please! There's something I've just got to go and do now. It won't take long and I'll come right back. Please, Dad."

Colin Renfrew looked down into his son's eyes. He'd never seen them more urgent, more pleading.

"What's going on, Callum?" he frowned.

"It's nothing, honest," Callum insisted. "I've just promised to be somewhere. I'll explain when I get back."

Callum's dad considered him for a moment. "You most certainly will," he said. But he didn't want an argument. Not out here in the street. And certainly not in front of Philip Bryce.

"Kids!" he muttered, shaking his head doubtfully. "All right, you've got fifteen minutes. Not a second more."

"No," growled Philip Bryce. "You're not going anywhere. Any of you. This has something to do with Jamie and I want to know where he is."

In spite of himself, Callum's dad looked faintly amused.

"Oh dear," he said, "have you gone and lost Jamie?"

Then he jerked his head indicating that Callum and his friends should just go.

"Fifteen minutes, remember," he warned.

The four children were already running up the road. As they disappeared, Colin couldn't resist chuckling to himself. Philip Bryce fixed him with a cold glare.

"I don't find anything remotely funny in this."

"Don't you?" Colin replied, still grinning. "I was just thinking. Philip Bryce. The hot shot businessman...who can't even control his own son."

On a hill outside the village, Jamie's eyes were fixed on the spot in the distance where the footpath across the field emerged from under the trees. They shouldn't be long now. Callum had said Abby and Megan were going to get him out of the house. He'd sounded so certain and with Max there to help, nothing could go wrong...could it?

Jamie's mind whirled around the possibilities.

Supposing the twins' plan hadn't worked. For all he knew, Callum might still be stuck indoors. Even if he had got out, his dad might have spotted all four of them as he drove like a maniac through the village. And Jamie couldn't even bring himself to think where that might lead.

No. Any minute now they'd be here. They had to be.

"All on your own, then?"

At the sound of the voice, Jamie spun round.

The stranger was sitting on the ground, his back up against the rusted iron shell of the old barn. He was early.

"My friends are on their way!" Jamie shouted. "They'll be here any minute. I've told them the truth and they believe me. Anyway, there's nothing you can do. It's not five o'clock yet."

"Jamie," the man said soothingly, gazing at his own slender toes sticking out from his open sandals, "you misunderstand. I'm not here to *do* anything. I'm what you might call a referee. I've come to see fair play."

"Is that what this is to you?" Jamie snapped. "Some sort of game?"

"Of course it is," smiled the man blandly. "There you were, a young lad who'd dug a bit of a hole for himself with his stories, and there I was with a solution. All I did was offer you the dice. You were the one who chose to throw it."

"But you didn't explain it properly," Jamie argued. "I didn't understand what I was getting into."

The man shrugged. "You understood enough to think you'd found a way to save your skin."

"No!" Jamie exploded. "This wasn't my fault. I thought you were mad! Anyway you made it sound like a good thing!"

"No more excuses, Jamie," the man sighed, shaking his head. "The truth is, no good ever comes of lying. It's too dangerous a game."

Jamie's head was beginning to spin. He couldn't think straight. Whatever he said, the man had an answer. In desperation, he turned back to study the footpath for any sign of his friends.

There was nothing. Just a slight ruffling of the grass as a breeze explored the hillside.

15

Countdown

"Eight minutes to five. Not looking very promising, is it?"

The seconds were ticking by and the man's voice was soft. Expressionless. It was as if he was just sitting waiting for the five o'clock deadline, the moment when Jamie's lies would finally get the better of him and he'd be stuck with them forever. He made Jamie want to spit.

"They'll be here," he murmured, as much to himself as to the man. "I know they'll be here."

But suddenly Jamie felt as if he knew nothing.

He kept his eyes fixed on the trees at the bottom of the field. Where were they? Something must have gone wrong, must have held them up.

Or there was that other possibility that had begun to gnaw away at the back of his mind. Perhaps they'd simply decided they didn't believe him after all.

"If you say so," sighed the man. "It's just that I can't help wondering what difference it really makes."

Jamie turned on him.

"What do you mean?" he demanded. "It makes all

the difference! It means I can go home."

The stranger raised his eyebrows and gazed into the distance thoughtfully.

"Tell me something, Jamie," he continued. "What if your friends do turn up? Just because they believe you, does that make you any less of a liar?"

He looked up into Jamie's angry, distrustful eyes.

"Why don't you give it up, all this business of trying to get back to your old life? Once a liar, always a liar. You and I both know this is where you belong."

There was something mesmerising in the stranger's face and voice. It was as if he was trying to seep inside Jamie's mind, confusing him, dragging him deep into a place he didn't want to go. Maybe the man was right. Maybe it would be easier to give in, to admit defeat and accept that there was no way out because, in the end, Jamie *was* just a liar. And he'd never be able to escape from himself.

He looked the man full in the face. He seemed to be seeing him properly for the first time. Everything about him was sharp and unforgiving – his nose, his lips, his chin, the long, bony fingers locked together in his lap. But most of all his eyes, which were studying Jamie minutely through narrow, lined slits that seemed too small for them.

And suddenly Jamie knew the stranger was trying to trick him.

"No! No, you're wrong!" he blurted out furiously. "This *isn't* where I belong. I've changed! I don't want to pretend anymore. I don't want to be something I'm not. And you know what? I'm not afraid of you and I'm not afraid to tell the truth!"

The man gave a vague, mocking smile.

"Brave words, Jamie, I'm impressed," he replied smoothly. "But when you get home, when you feel safe again back with your boring old dad, can you honestly say that you'll risk everything and tell your friends the truth about yourself? Back there, they still think you're a rich kid."

"Whatever happens," Jamie promised, "I'm not hiding anything anymore. I'll never tell another lie as long as I live."

Almost at once, the man sprang to his feet gleefully and clapped his hands together.

"Good for you!" he cried. "So, as far as I can make out, there's only one problem."

The glittering eyes disappeared even further as the corners of his mouth twisted upwards into their cruel smile.

"There's no sign of your friends," he sneered, "and...it's five minutes to five."

For a split second, Jamie sensed a heaving wave of despair about to come crashing down on him.

The man was right. They were nowhere to be seen.

As far as he was concerned, Jamie had lost and he'd won.

"JAMIE!"

It came out of nowhere. A frantic shout, hurtling across the field towards him.

Callum!

Jamie whirled round and there they were, red-faced, hot and breathless. The four missing pieces. The four friends who believed in him because that's exactly what they were – his friends!

"You see!" Jamie cried. He was so relieved he was almost laughing. "I told you they'd come. I told you!"

"Indeed you did," was the quiet response. "What a pity."

Jamie looked round uneasily. The man was standing close behind him. His eyes seemed to have shrunk to little more than glistening gashes in his face. Jamie didn't like him being so near. It made his skin creep.

But the sight of his friends blasted all the lies out of his head, and he began to wave at them excitedly.

"I should calm down if I were you," the stranger warned. "We're not quite done yet."

"Of course we are!" Jamie answered, pointing down the hill. "They've come, haven't they? That means they believe me. And anyway, *you're* here.

When they see you they'll know I've been telling the truth."

The man stared at him in surprise.

"Oh, Jamie," he said, "is that what you're relying on?"

Then, as if he couldn't help himself, his face suddenly crumpled and he laughed delightedly.

"Well, I'm sorry to disappoint you but…they won't see me. They *can't* see me! I'm not part of their world. This is *your* lie, not theirs!"

WHAT?

It was as though all the air had been punched out of him. Jamie gazed at the man, horrified. He'd managed to climb out of one deep, dark hole only to crash straight down into another.

He looked back at the four figures racing up the hill towards them. Towards *him*! He was the only one they could see. How would he explain this? Could he honestly expect them to believe that they'd never see the stranger he'd been telling them about because apparently, for them, he didn't exist? How much further could he push them? Not this far, he was sure.

Callum was the first to reach him.

"You've no idea what we've been through to get here!" he gasped.

The others stumbled breathlessly across the grass,

glancing around eagerly for any sign of the man Jamie was supposed to meet. Jamie couldn't look at them.

Callum saw his face and frowned.

"What is it? Are we too late?"

Jamie's eyes were fixed on the ground, but he knew the man was watching him. Still smiling. Enjoying every wretched moment.

"Jamie?" Max puffed. "Jamie, what's going on?"

He got barely a shrug in response.

Abby's face fell as the disappointment swept over her.

"He's gone, hasn't he?" she mumbled hopelessly. "We've missed him."

Jamie shook his head. "No, you haven't missed him," he said, knowing it was pointless, but saying it anyway. "He's right here. He's standing beside me."

His voice was empty. Quiet. And as he glanced up, he saw it instantly – the look of mistrust that flashed into Callum's eyes.

"What do you mean, he's right here?" Callum asked cautiously, looking all around. "There's no-one."

The man leaned in towards Jamie, a gaunt cheek brushing his ear.

"Come on then, Jamie, let's have it," he whispered. "Let's hear how you're going to explain your way out of this one."

But Jamie knew there was nothing left to say. Not any more. He'd seen Callum's expression change. Whatever belief he had in Jamie must have been hanging by a wisp. And it had just snapped.

"I hate to hurry you," smirked the man, "but you've only got two minutes left. Why don't we just skip it, eh?"

He placed a cold, spindly hand on Jamie's rigid shoulder, then added, "Welcome to your new home!"

It was like setting off an explosion.

Jamie spun round. His right arm flailed out, knocking the man's hand away. Then he shoved him, ramming his hands into his chest so hard that, with one violent push, he sent his thin body sprawling onto the grass before he had a chance to defend himself.

"This is not my home!" Jamie screamed down at him. "This will never be my home! You're a cheat. You suck people in then you sit back and enjoy it while things get totally messed up. Yes, I've told some lies. Yes, I've done the wrong thing. But however bad I am, I will never be as evil as you!"

He paused for a moment. He was breathing heavily. Everything was draining away. His whole life.

"Let's face it," he added bitterly, "you've wanted me to fail from the start. I never stood a chance."

Before the man could answer, Callum lunged

forward.

"Have you completely lost it?" he yelled in Jamie's face, his disappointment boiling over. "Do you really think that throwing yourself around and having daft conversations with nobody is going to swing it for you? I don't know which of us is the saddest – you for trying it on or us for believing you!"

Jamie hung his head miserably. He didn't have the energy left to argue.

"You can believe me or not, Callum," he murmured, "it's up to you. It's probably too late now anyway."

As he spoke, Jamie was suddenly aware of curious shadows beginning to flicker across Callum's furious face. He turned his head sharply.

And there it was.

The Lying Tree must have slid silently out of the ground while they were talking. Now it stood darkly against the decaying skin of the old barn. Its branches, dressed in their sinister, greenish-black, stretched out towards Jamie as if trying to grasp him in some hideous embrace.

Beside it, the man had picked himself up and was brushing grass off his sleeves. He may have been taken off guard by Jamie's attack, but he wasn't going to allow it to spoil his moment of victory.

"My, my, what a temper you have," he said, his

voice maddeningly calm. "Still, I suppose I can't blame you. It must be very annoying to have to admit defeat. Especially when you've been trying so hard."

He sighed, then added briskly, "Still, time waits for no man. And here's my tree. Right on cue."

Suddenly, Megan pushed Callum out of the way.

"This can't be it, Jamie!" she shrieked, her eyes pleading with him. "It just can't be, I won't let it be. Not after everything you've told us. After everything we've done to get here. You said you could save our house. We believed you. Tell me we weren't wrong to do that."

Jamie felt so helpless he couldn't speak. But Megan grabbed hold of him and began to shake him furiously.

"Tell me!"

Behind him, the man sniggered.

Whether it was the sickening sound of his mocking laughter or the desperation in Megan's voice that gave Jamie the jolt he needed, he had no idea. But in an instant he'd decided.

He was going to get out. He was going to get them all out.

"No, Megan, you weren't wrong," he spluttered. "None of you were wrong. You believed me before so believe me now and we can all get home."

He turned to look at the stranger.

"The man I met is here. I'm looking right at him. I know you can't see him. That's because it's *my* lies that have got us here, not yours. The tree is here too but you can't see that either. None of it makes any sense, I know, but if things are ever going to get back to normal you've got to trust me. Just this one last time."

There was silence. Max was watching him intently. In Jamie's earnest expression he could still see exactly what he'd seen the day before: total belief in what he was saying. And if Jamie believed it, it had to be the truth...didn't it?

"One last time?" Max murmured finally. "All right. I'll believe you. One last time."

Jamie could feel a surge of energy blast through his body. He saw Max look at the twins.

There was only a moment's hesitation. Then Abby nodded.

"Me too."

"And me," Megan added quietly.

Callum said nothing. Max took a step towards him.

"Come on, Cal," he begged. "Once more."

An ugly, satisfied smile was beginning to creep across the man's face.

"Nice try, Jamie," he sighed. "Pity it's too little too late. Time's up."

"No!" Jamie shouted. "Not when I'm this close!"

"The tree's ready for you, Jamie. All you have to do is touch the trunk and you'll seal our agreement."

Jamie swung round.

"Cal, please! We're almost there. But it's not going to happen if you won't believe me."

"Cal, you've got to do it," Max joined in, "it's all of us or none of us."

Callum glared at them. His head was throbbing. He didn't know what to think anymore.

"But why *should* I believe you?" he found himself yelling out.

"Because you're my best friends!" Jamie couldn't be any more honest than that. "You're my best friends and I don't want to lose you!"

As Jamie finished speaking, he was suddenly aware of an uneasy silence beginning to steal across the hillside. Even the breeze had dropped. It was like the quiet before a storm. But the sky above him was a cloudless blue. There wasn't a storm coming.

In the pit of his stomach, something peculiar was happening. It felt as if he was being sucked backwards from the inside. The next moment, his feet were losing their grip on the grass. He tensed himself to try to keep his balance. Then he realised to his horror that he was sliding backwards. In one ghastly instant, he seemed to have lost control of his body!

The tree was clawing him in!

He looked round frantically. Callum was closest.

"Cal, help me!" he screamed, and reached out to grasp his friend's jacket with both hands. The pulling behind him was growing stronger, dragging him further backwards inch by inch.

Callum just stood looking at him. Had he even noticed what was going on? Or was this something else he simply couldn't see?

The man stepped into Jamie's line of vision.

"You're wasting your time, Jamie," he said. "The seven-day trial's over. As I said, the tree's ready for you. I'm afraid you're here to stay."

The smile of triumph was once again on his lips, and the tips of the tree's branches were already beginning to push into Jamie's back.

"All right, I believe you!"

Callum's voice rang out through the stillness. The man whipped round angrily.

"What?" Jamie gasped.

"I said I believe you, deaf-ears! So let's get out of here!"

Jamie felt the flood of relief as it swept over him. He looked over expectantly at the stranger. But the man was just standing, motionless. Across his face the papery, yellow skin seemed stretched so tightly it looked almost transparent.

In that same moment, Jamie realised he hadn't stopped moving. The tree was still dragging him backwards! Was that it, then? Was it too late? No! It couldn't be. Not now he'd got Callum back. He had to give it one final try.

He opened his mouth and yelled at the top of his voice. "Then pull me!"

Callum looked incredulous.

"*Now* what are you talking about?" he demanded.

"If you want to get home, pull me!" screamed Jamie. "And do it NOW!"

Callum stared at him.

"You're barking mad, Jamie Bryce," he muttered.

But his hands closed around Jamie's wrists anyway and he began to pull. To his surprise, Jamie didn't move. Callum could see nothing, but he felt the resistance. It was as if Jamie's body was locked solid to something. Callum frowned and heaved harder.

A sharp pain shot across Jamie's shoulders. He thought his arms would be wrenched out of their sockets.

"Callum, please!" he howled.

As he glanced helplessly behind him, he saw the tree's trunk getting nearer and nearer. In seconds his back would be flat against it. And once his body touched it, it would all be over.

Jamie was frantic. Desperately he dug in his heels,

struggling to get a foothold in the grass. Callum's grip on his wrists was painfully fierce. But he couldn't stop. He squeezed his eyes tight shut, strained forward against the tree's powerful pull. Any moment now...

Then suddenly, miraculously, something gave! Jamie felt the instant of release. He took in a sharp gasp of breath, then hurtled forward into Callum like a piece of snapped elastic. The two of them crashed to the ground.

Max and the twins watched in stunned silence. It was the oddest thing they'd ever seen.

"Thanks, Jamie," Callum groaned. "I think you've broken my back."

Jamie didn't reply. He just lay quite still. Was that it? Was it over?

But when he raised his head, the man was still there, staring down at him. He might have been cut out of wax.

"Well, well, this is a surprise," the stranger said, so quietly that Jamie guessed the words on his lips more than heard them. "Who would have thought they'd believe in you that much?"

Then he smiled. As cold and distant as he had ever been.

"Still, we know the truth, don't we?"

His mouth moved only once more. The shape it

made was unmistakeable.

"Liar."

It took the man just three steps to get over to the tree. Four to push through the eagerly waiting branches. Jamie tried to peer in but the covering of leaves was too dense. He couldn't see the man anymore.

For one last second he gazed at the tree, the next it was wrapped in a huge, squirming ball of flames that shot upwards to the sky. The heat was so intense he had to hold up his arms to shield his face.

Then it was gone.

Where the tree had stood, there was nothing.

Flat against the ground, Jamie found himself shaking, struggling to catch his breath. He managed to roll over, half afraid even to look around him. There was no-one there.

Shadows were beginning to stretch long fingers across the hillside and Jamie was alone.

16

Game over

Philip Bryce sat in his office ignoring the piece of
paper at his elbow scribbled with a list of names and
phone numbers; people he was supposed to ring,
appointments he needed to make. It had been a
surprising day. Not bad really, but difficult. He held a
letter between his fingers. The contents had been
troubling him since he'd opened it that morning.

But it wasn't the letter that caught his attention
now. It was the photograph in the silver frame on his
desk of his son, Jamie. He was standing by the front
door in his new school uniform. Philip Bryce had
taken the picture on the spur of the moment on
Jamie's first day at Wellbridge Primary, and it was a
good one. There was a lot of his mum in that half-
smiling, half-anxious face. He was a great kid.
Whatever problems there were between them weren't
Jamie's fault. He was just a boy and lately life had
been tough on him.

But Jamie seemed to have coped. He seemed to
have dealt with all of it. Only now that this letter had
arrived, Philip Bryce couldn't help wondering, would

he really be able to handle this too?

There was an unexpected knock at the door. It annoyed him. The last thing he wanted was to be interrupted. Not right now. There were days when he wished the world would just leave him alone. This was one of them.

Jamie knocked for a second time.

"Dad? Are you there?"

Jamie's was the last voice his dad was expecting to hear.

"Jamie?" he spluttered. "Sorry, yes, come in," and he hastily stuffed the letter back into its envelope and slid it into the top drawer of his desk.

His son stood in the doorway looking at him. There was something in his expression his dad had never seen before. He stood up, faintly alarmed.

"What is it, Jamie? What's wrong?"

Jamie had cycled off to school before the post arrived that morning. He couldn't possibly know about the letter. Unless...

His dad felt a coldness creep over him. Unless a letter had been sent to Jamie at school. Or there had been a phone call.

"Come on, Jamie," he said gently, "tell me what's happened."

"Nothing's happened," Jamie answered, "I just...I just wanted to see you."

He tried to smile but instead a sob caught in his throat and tears of relief began streaming down his cheeks. His dad stepped out from behind his desk and, before he realised what was happening, Jamie's arms were clamped around his waist in a hug that almost squeezed all the breath out of him. He was so taken aback that his own arms remained sticking awkwardly out to the sides, as if he didn't know what to do with them. It'd been years since they'd shared a hug.

Then suddenly they closed tenderly around the skinny eleven-year-old who had jammed himself into him.

"I've missed you, Dad," Jamie blurted out without thinking. "I've missed you so much."

His dad was puzzled. "What do you mean? I only saw you this morning."

Jamie shuddered slightly, still trying to get control of the sobs shaking his body. He lifted his head and looked up into his dad's kind but baffled face.

And then Jamie understood.

This past week of his life hadn't existed here. His dad had got up that morning and gone to work, and, as far as he was concerned, Jamie was simply calling in to see him at the estate agents after school. There had been no panic. No massive police search. There had been nothing on the news because there was no news to tell.

A single day. That's all that had passed.

A smile began to spread across Jamie's face. No explanations were needed because there were no questions to be asked. All that mattered was that the other Philip Bryce was gone. Quite simply he didn't exist anymore. Jamie was back where he belonged, and for the first time in his life he was so grateful to be there.

Half an hour later, his dad was unlocking the front door of number 15 Deal Street. The house didn't look tatty anymore. It looked like home. As Jamie kicked off his trainers in the porch, his dad glanced down at them and shook his head.

"Those really are getting very old. How about we go and sort out a new pair tomorrow?"

Jamie looked down at the worn out shoes – the broken, knotted lace of one, the sole coming away from the other – and smiled.

"No, it's fine. I really like these."

In the kitchen, the table hadn't been cleared from breakfast.

"Sorry, Jamie, I didn't get a chance to wash up this morning," Jamie's dad murmured apologetically. "Something came in the post. I had to deal with it."

"Don't worry about it," Jamie chuckled. "It's only a few dishes."

He was about to take his bag upstairs when his dad stopped him.

"Jamie," he began slowly, "there's something I have to talk to you about."

Jamie turned and grabbed his moment.

"There's something I have to talk to you about too," he said. "Can I do it now?"

His dad hesitated.

"Go on then," he sighed. He'd waited all day for this. He could wait a little longer. "But afterwards I need you to listen to me, all right?"

Now it was Jamie's turn to hesitate. "You won't get cross, will you?"

"Why should I get cross?"

"Because I've done something wrong."

The shadow of a frown passed across his dad's face.

"Go on."

"I didn't mean to," Jamie faltered. "At least, I *did* mean to, but it all went wrong. It got sort of out of hand."

"Whatever it is, I'm sure it can't be all that bad."

"It is though," Jamie insisted. "I've been telling lies to my friends. Ever since we moved here. I've been telling them we have lots of money and we live in a really big, posh house. I've made up this whole life for us."

He paused. This next part was much harder to admit.

"And I told them stuff about Mum."

Jamie's dad's eyes were suddenly very serious.

"Like what?" he wanted to know.

"I said she never left," Jamie managed to say. "I just pretended she worked away a lot."

There was no response.

"I'm sorry, Dad. That's why I've never asked anyone round. If I did they'd find out the truth. I didn't mean to lie, I just didn't want them to know about me."

His dad thought for a moment then asked quietly, "What is it about you that you didn't want them to know?"

For the second time that afternoon, the tears welled up in Jamie's tired eyes.

"That I wasn't good enough for her," he sobbed. "For Mum. That she didn't want me enough to stay."

"Oh, Jamie!"

Once again, Jamie's dad's arms were wrapped tightly around him. "Is that what you think? Is that what's been in your head all this time?"

"Well, what else am I supposed to think?" Jamie snapped. "You never talk about her. You never said why she'd gone."

"Why ever she went, it had nothing to do with you.

It was to do with me. With *her* and with *me*. Not you. She loves you. She'll always love you."

"But why don't you ever talk about her?" Jamie went on. "Sometimes all I want to do is just *talk* to you about her."

For a moment Jamie's dad didn't know what to say. How could he have been so wrong?

"When your mum left," he sighed finally, "I thought the best way to deal with it was to try and make things as normal for you as possible. I thought that if we didn't really talk about her, if we moved away from the life she'd been part of, then gradually she wouldn't be so important to you. Maybe you'd forget about her."

As the words tumbled out of his mouth and he looked down into his son's bewildered face, he couldn't believe how stupid he'd been.

"How could I forget her?" Jamie exclaimed. "She's my mum."

His dad hung his head.

"I'm sorry, Jamie, I thought you were dealing with it."

Jamie sniffed and nodded.

"All right, your turn. You said there was something you wanted to say to me, too."

To Jamie's surprise, his dad gave an odd laugh. But then he stopped and frowned. Clearly *his* news was going to be difficult to explain too.

"Funnily enough," he said at last, "it's about your mum. I've been worrying about this all day. Should I tell you, shouldn't I tell you? Is it really right to drag it all up again?"

He gave his son a squeeze.

"But you can't drag something up again if it's never gone away in the first place, can you?"

Jamie was puzzled. "I don't know what you mean."

His dad sat back and considered him for a moment thoughtfully. Then he seemed to come to a decision. He reached into his pocket and took out an envelope. It was addressed to P. Bryce, 15 Deal Street.

"I've had a letter," he murmured. "It came this morning. It's from your mum." Jamie's eyes grew huge.

"She wants to visit, Jamie," he heard his dad announce. "She wants to see you."

Never had Jamie's own rumpled bed been so welcome as it was that night. It was late. Nearly eleven o'clock. But there had been so much to talk about. The time had flown.

There would be a lot to talk about tomorrow too. His dad was going to drive him to Wellbridge where Jamie was meeting up with Max, Abby, Megan and Callum. He was going to tell them all about himself.

The truth. It was time to try and explain the lies.

Later, he'd invite them all back to Deal Street and his small, terraced house. He wasn't ashamed of it anymore. Or of his dad. Of course his friends might not want to come. They might not want to know him when they found out what lies he'd been telling them.

But at least he'd have been honest. For the first time in months, he could be himself.

As Jamie went to turn off his light, his attention was caught by something in his wastepaper basket. He stretched forward and tilted it towards him to get a better look.

In the bottom of the basket lay a leaf. A leaf with six points.

Jamie hadn't a clue how it could have got there. He reached in slowly and lifted it out. It wasn't fresh and green as it had been when he'd last seen it. It was black and charred and thin as cheap paper.

And as Jamie turned it over, it crumbled to pieces in his hands.